Airship Daedalus
The Arctic Menace

By Todd Downing

FIRST EDITION

ISBN: 978-1-7349293-0-0

Copyright © 2019 Todd Downing & Deep7 Press

All Rights Reserved Worldwide

Edited by Dan Heinrich & Andrea Edelman

Sensitivity reader Devielle Johnson

Cover art & design by Todd Downing
(*Daedalus* model by Hans Piwenitzky)

Based on the *Airship Daedalus / AEGIS Tales* setting and characters by Todd Downing and published in various media by Deep7 Press. *Airship Daedalus*™ and *AEGIS Tales*™ are trademarks of Deep7 Press.

WWW.AIRSHIPDAEDALUS.COM

Deep7 Press is a subsidiary of Despot Media, LLC
1214 Woods Rd SE Port Orchard, WA 98366 USA
WWW.DEEP7.COM

PRINTED IN USA

In memory of my grandparents,
Jack & Dorothy.

- CHAPTER 1 -

Los Angeles, September 1928

The two-year-old surplus biplane banked left, completing its circle above the foothills of Newhall, the rural suburb of Santa Clarita that ran from Quigley Canyon east to Pico Canyon west. A patchwork quilt of duns, greens, and browns spread out below, the estates and ranches of old-money Spanish families and the film industry elite.

The whole region was shifting: formerly a quiet, agrarian collection of orange groves and walnut orchards, now home to the burgeoning movie business, and the celebrities who made it run.

Jack McGraw sat in the rear crew compartment, controlling the plane with the secondary stick and throttle, the rear cowling arched across his back like the frame of a chair. He was a strapping six-footer and change, broad shoulders almost comically sprouting from the top of the cockpit, just above the jaunty title painted in gold on the rear fuselage: "CAPTAIN STRATOSPHERE".

Dressed in well-worn flight gear of brown leather, complete with cap and Resistal goggles, his clean-shaven jaw worked a stick of Black Jack licorice chewing gum with all the subtlety of a meat tenderizer.

In the front compartment sat nine-year-old Ellen Starr, stray locks of strawberry hair sprouting from her own leather flight cap, crystal blue eyes gazing out from her own Resistal lenses. She too chewed a piece of gum, though her choice was Beeman's wintergreen.

It was no surprise that Ellen bore a striking resemblance to Jack at the same age. She was the product of a love affair between Jack and a battlefield nurse, Dorothy Brown, with whom he had spent a furlough in Paris toward the end of the war. In a display of uncharacteristic practicality, Dorothy had broken Jack's heart. A pilot with the RAF No. 32 Squadron —which was rife with Jack's American countrymen—his life expectancy wasn't great, nor were his prospects if he survived.

Dorothy had gone back to her field surgeon sweetheart, eventually getting married and setting up house in New Jersey. Jack had gone back to the war, back to his life. After the Armistice, he'd remained in Europe, getting into a few scrapes with Italian fascists before returning home to the US. Pushing thirty, itinerant, with little to show for his life, he'd become a professional test pilot for the burgeoning aeronautics industry.

That's when Dorothy had come back into his life.

She hadn't aged a day in the seven years they'd been apart, although he soon found out that life had been extraordinarily unkind to her during that time. She'd earned her medical diploma and started a family, but had been tragically widowed. Dorothy worked for AEGIS, the A of which stood for "American" at the time. A philanthropic concern funded by the titans of industry, it was headed by its cofounder, Thomas Edison. Her late husband had died on assignment for the organization in South America.

Dorothy recruited Jack to lead a crew of his former war buddies against a paramilitary occult organization called the *Astrum Argentum*, or Silver Star, ruled by the sinister magus Aleister Crowley, who was bent on conquest by arcane means.

Together they'd flown around the world at least once, battling the forces of the Silver Star in all manner of exotic locales, championing the ethics of good over evil, order over chaos.

At the end of their first mission to the Caribbean and the sweltering Amazon jungle,

Dorothy—now known as "Doc" among the crew—had revealed her daughter's true parentage to Jack.

Until that moment in the lobby of the U.S. Grant Hotel in San Diego three years ago, Jack McGraw had been a rudderless ship, adrift on whatever seas life saw fit to throw his way. But since meeting Ellen, and discovering his relationship to her, he'd become a different man. Nurturing. Motivated. Fully engaged with his new family.

Doc still put off making anything official, and that was okay by Jack. As long as she and Ellen were in his life, and he in theirs, he could be content.

The plane was a Fleetwing racing and mail service prototype made by the Pitcairn Aircraft Company of Willow Grove, Pennsylvania, which McGraw had purchased from the company at a fraction of its value, thanks to his reputation as a Great War ace and a celebrity adventurer. His ties to the Allied Enterprise Group for International Security didn't hurt, either.

It had a sleek body with two control cockpits, the original third passenger compartment having been removed in favor of a much larger powerplant. A Packard 1a-1500 air-cooled engine roared behind its spinning propeller, late afternoon sun gleaming off the fire engine red body and chrome cowling. The disparately oversized engine made the short fuselage nose-heavy, but Jack easily justified the extra challenge in flight control for the greater boost in speed. Flying this kite was like riding a pony with the ferocity of a bucking bronco.

Its registry was simply PA-1X, and it had crashed during testing when the flight controls had been rigged backwards by accident. Jack had flown all kinds of planes, from all manner of nations; he had a special place in his heart for Curtiss aircraft, but had to admit he didn't mind taking a gorgeous prototype such as the PA-1X off the manufacturer's hands at a steal of a price. It allowed him the chance to rebuild her from the wheels up.

Jack leveled the plane and let himself take in the view. Below them stretched the community of Newhall, with its affluent craftsman bungalows and occasional Spanish mansions. Across the railroad tracks and Newhall Avenue stretched the entirety of the San Fernando Valley, lush and green.

There was almost no trace left of the catastrophic flood that past March, a failure of the St. Francis dam, which had killed almost six-hundred residents. It was a resilient community full of bootstrappers and self-mades, and they'd rebuilt with a ferocity that bordered on abject defiance of nature. Directly south lay the rural expanse of Topanga, and beyond that, the Pacific Ocean. Jack could smell the salt air on the breeze, noting the sun hanging low in the west.

But the brilliant orange glow of the late afternoon sky over the Pacific didn't concern him. Their destination was far closer: the Starr-McGraw Ranch, a 200-acre retreat nestled in the hills above Wildwood Canyon. The property abutted the southern border of silent Western film star William S. Hart's *La Loma de los Vientos*—The Hill of the Winds—also known simply as "Horseshoe Ranch" by the locals.

Although the new breed of action cowboys like Tom Mix had taken much of his box office, the 64-year-old Hart wasn't to be counted out, not by a long shot. At Horseshoe, he could write his books, care for his ill sister, and do all the producer work it took to get pictures made.

Ellen pressed the *TALK* mechanism on her radio headset collar. "Can we buzz Mr. Hart's house?" she asked with a mischievous gleam in her eye that Jack couldn't see, but could absolutely imagine.

McGraw knew the cowboy star could usually be found working outside at this time of day, either tending his horses, clearing brush, or landscaping near the pristine white stucco of his Spanish Colonial Revival mansion. Jack liked Bill Hart, found him a gracious and friendly neighbor. But he also enjoyed some good-natured fun, and relished any opportunity to instruct Ellen in the finer points of barnstorming.

"Stick's all yours, Red," Jack replied through the radio. "Keep her level. Remember the nose is heavy."

"Affirmative," Ellen grinned, leaning forward on the stick, as she throttled to full speed.

Jack felt his guts leap into his throat as the plane dropped low over the town, the red tile roofs and wooden store facades zipping by under them. In less than three seconds, they were across the tracks, across Newhall Avenue, and coming in fast over Bill Hart's property.

As expected, Hart was harvesting some late blooms from a collection of rose bushes beside the mansion, and he glanced up at the growl of the Packard engine as the plane bore down over his yard.

Ellen tipped the right wings upward in salute and screamed a war cry as she sped past, the wake of wind pulling Hart's cowboy hat from his head.

He coughed a bit of dust from his tight line of a mouth, squinting after the aircraft as it headed south and cleared his property line. "That girl," he mumbled. Wandering on slender, saddle-worn legs to retrieve his hat, he squinted at the low sun and slapped the Stetson against his leg to dust it off. Then, chuckling, he returned to his roses.

The plane suddenly dropped as it cleared the plateau over the canyon, and Jack's gut instinct was to take the stick, but he held off, waiting to see what Ellen would do. An experienced pilot might have anticipated the strange air currents within the dips, crags, and eddies of the locale, but Ellen was still learning. She pulled back on the stick, nosing the Fleetwing upward, while applying a bit more throttle to compensate for the sudden loss of altitude. It was the right call. Jack grinned silently behind her, proud of her reasoning and developing skill.

"Okay, kiddo," he said into the radio, "taking the stick. Prepare for landing."

"Yessir, Cap'n," she saluted. It was a broad gesture intended to get his attention, and he laughed.

Banking a hard left, Jack circled over Quigley Canyon to set up for his final approach. Flaps shifted and the two pilots leaned with the G-force of the maneuver. They could see the ranch beneath them: the sprawling main house a white stucco example of the Spanish architecture so popular among the residents of Southern California; the converted barn that functioned as a full-service airplane hangar and automotive garage; the nearby outbuildings which housed Jack's ever-growing collection of vehicles; the orchard of walnuts and apricots; the large, rectangular swimming pool surrounded by a massive brick patio; the two small telephone shacks stationed at the southern corners of the property, which doubled as barracks for security personnel on duty.

The runway was a gravel strip lying north-south near the southern property line. Jack and Ellen watched as their plateau fell away into the expanse of the canyon. They would make another turn, cut speed, and come in from the south.

Ellen pinched the *TALK* button again. "Immelmann? Please?"

"Really, Red?" came Jack's skeptical reply. "Remember what happened last time?"

"I won't puke this time, I promise!"

That was all the encouragement Jack needed. "Okay then. Hold onto your butt."

Pulling back on the stick, Jack braced himself as the Fleetwing rocketed upward, shooting into the orange sky. Just when he heard the engine begin to sputter and stall, he applied full rudder and yawed the plane over in a backward corkscrew.

This particular "wingover" maneuver was named for German fighter pilot Max Immelmann, who had developed it during the Great War to maximize his options after an attack. It required extreme precision on the part of the pilot, due to the aircraft's slow speed. The updrafts from the canyon and the plane's nose weight made it even more tricky.

Jack had performed it only a handful of times during the war, but many times since, and it never failed to send a thrill to every part of his body.

Ellen squealed and giggled with delight, feeling the world tumble upside down, taking her stomach with it. She was a child well-loved and well-cared-for. Her mother presided over her academics, steeping her in history, mathematics, and occult lore. Those lessons were supplemented by her great aunts, Millie and Agnes, who had toured the world with her, twice over, before her sixth birthday. Her father filled in all the practical knowledge she'd need to meet her full potential in a bold new age: riding, shooting, mechanics, and of course, flying.

The nose of the Fleetwing dropped, and the gravel landing strip loomed up from below. Jack cut the throttle to bare minimum, letting the plane glide down on the late afternoon breeze. The two front wheels bounced once on contact, then spun forward under the weight of the airplane. Jack set all flaps to their upright braking position, coming to a rolling stop a hundred feet later.

To the right of the runway sat a familiar blue Curtiss XA-2, the signature plane of Wanda "Wings" Jensen, fellow stunt pilot and AEGIS field agent. She and Jack had done some aerial stunt work for a few movies together, including the recent war picture that bore her nickname.

"Hey, Aunt Wanda's here!" Ellen shouted, not bothering with the headset.

Jack pinched the *TALK* control on his collar. "Why don't you hop out and go say hi. I'll put the plane to bed and join you for dinner."

The young girl didn't need further instruction. Leaping from the front cockpit, Ellen cleared the fuselage and made it to the ground with a single intermediate jump to the lower wing. Then she was off toward the main house, and Jack throttled forward, steering the Fleetwing with its foot controls.

The plane bobbled across the edge of the gravel landing strip, rolling in a gradual left turn toward the hangar. As he approached, the landscaped circular drive near the front of the house became visible, and Jack could see a maroon Cadillac sedan from the previous model year parked out front. They were apparently having all sorts of company this evening.

As he pulled to a stop and cut the engine, a dark-haired lad of eighteen strolled from the auto garage to meet him. Jason Jefferson was of average height, with a stocky build. His chestnut eyes were closely set on a broad face, and his ubiquitous smile displayed a proud gap in his upper teeth.

An orphan from birth, he was what most folks referred to as "slow", but Jack had seen him rebuild a carburetor for an electric generator on a movie set in about five minutes flat, and had offered him a job on the spot. "Jinx"—a moniker of his own choosing—got fifty dollars a week plus room and board, just to keep the McGraw collection of motor vehicles in working order. As the jazz musicians on The Avenue would say, it was a "choice gig".

Jack slid from the rear pilot's compartment and leaped to the ground. "Who's with the Caddy?" he asked, nodding at the parked car in the front drive.

"Some lady," Jinx shrugged, wiping his hands on an oily rag and tucking it into the back pocket of his coveralls. "Never seen her before."

Jack took up position on the left, Jinx on the right, and together they pushed the Fleetwing into the cavernous barn.

"How's the engine rebuild coming on Doc's Ford?"

"Soon, Captain," Jinx grunted as they heaved their weight behind the lower wings. "Done when it's done."

"Can't argue with that," said Jack.

"Got a lead on a Boeing XP-4 if you're interested. Might fit this Packard engine better."

"Really? Gee, that's tempting, Jinx," Jack admitted. "Sure, we can chat about it later. But first I need to see who's paying us a call, and if it's got anything to do with Wings being here."

They pivoted the plane and backed it into a dedicated space on the dirt floor of the hangar, the massive engine clicking and pinging as it cooled.

Jack shucked his leather gloves and clapped Jinx on a broad shoulder. "No more work today, huh? Button up the barn and I'll see you back at the house for chow." He spat the well-chewed wad of gum into the ashcan by the left barn door.

Jinx saluted his patron, gapsome teeth in a wide smile. "Aye aye, Captain!"

- CHAPTER 2 -

The back door to the main house was buffered by a screen porch the family used as a mud room. As Jack entered, he could see the horizontal line of coat pegs at chest height running from the back door to the wall of wooden milk crates, stacked on their sides, used as cubbies for muddy shoes, oil-stained shirts, or any other article of clothing Doc deemed too dirty to enter the house.

The screen door clacked shut behind him, and he noticed a familiar brown leather jacket bearing an AEGIS Aeronautics patch on the shoulder hanging from one of the pegs. Wings was just over a year with the organization, assigned mostly to missions in the Southern California region. It wasn't unusual for her to drop in for the occasional dinner, as the Starr-McGraw clan was just about the only family she had anymore.

Jack shrugged out from his own leather jacket, hanging it on the peg next to hers, and stowed his flight cap, goggles, and gloves in a convenient cubby.

The main house was built in the same late Spanish colonial style as Bill Hart's mansion, though laid out in a more sprawling design. Exposed timbers erupted from textured stucco walls, creating a well-worn yet sturdy feel. The floors were ceramic tile of a ruddy brown hue, the decor a selection of Mission-style oak and leather pieces in complementary earth tones, often draped with wool blankets of woven southwestern or Mexican designs.

An Edison Diamond phonograph stood in the corner of the sunken family room, ensconced in an ornate walnut cabinet. The top was open, the seductive trill of Annette Hanshaw's new record, *I Must Have That Man*, wafting delightfully through the room to a peppy jazz cadence.

Jack smiled cordially as he entered, closing the door quietly behind him, and took a silent head count.

Ellen stood near Wings, describing her aerial adventures to the pilot in excited detail, complete with hand motions and sound effects. Wanda Jensen was slim and blond, dressed in dun-colored jodhpurs, black knee boots, and a gray cotton work shirt with the sleeves rolled at the elbows. She threw a subtle wink at Jack, then went back to listening to Ellen's riveting tale.

Doc stood leaning against the wrought-iron railing that ran up from the family room to the main level, bisecting the living space into two zones. Radiant emerald eyes and red bee-stung lips were set pleasingly in a heart-shaped face, framed by a curly dark chestnut bob which she'd allowed to grow out for the past four months.

In her forest-green skirt suit and brown Oxford heels, she was often compared to the young actress Myrna Loy, who had been cast to play her in the serialized adventures of the airship *Daedalus* crew. She held a highball glass Jack knew was a Gin Rickey, her current favorite cocktail, despite the 18th Amendment.

The woman standing next to Doc at the railing Jack didn't know, and she cast a discerning look in his direction. She was in her fifties, a plump five-foot-four, dressed in a maroon skirt and matching jacket, white cloche hat cupping a head of tightly-pinned black waves tinged with silver. Her face displayed miles of hard road through her olive complexion, dark brown eyes looking Jack up and down and noting everything in an instant.

"Ah," Doc greeted, "there you are."

Jack ascended the four-step stairway in two bounds, stopping beside Doc as she leaned in to kiss him gently on the lips. She handed the highball glass to him, and he took a sip.

"This is Mrs. Lucia Flores," Doc explained, nodding toward the visitor by way of introduction. "She's the new AEGIS bureau chief for the Southern California region."

The woman extended a manicured hand, and Jack shook it politely with a slight bow.

"Ma'am."

"I know it's late in the day, and you must be getting ready for supper," Lucia began, "but I'm afraid this can't wait. Can we speak privately?"

Wings stood from the sofa below, tousling Ellen's strawberry curls. "You go ahead. I'll get this monster cleaned up and meet you at the table."

Doc cracked a tiny smile, trying not to let her nervousness show through. "Okay, don't wait for us."

Jack gestured down the hall toward the front of the house. "This way," he said.

They crossed the main floor together and passed through a pair of French doors into a comfortable study that looked out onto the covered porch, topiary landscaping, and the circular drive beyond. Birch bookshelves stretched floor to ceiling, covering every wall but the front window and the double doors into the foyer.

A venerable oak desk dominated the center of the room, covered in a leather blotter, stacks of random notebooks and reference tomes, and a candlestick telephone. In the outer orbit of the study sat a selection of overstuffed leather chairs, and small end tables holding Tiffany stained-glass reading lamps.

The ladies entered ahead of Jack, who closed the doors behind them, going immediately to the desk to grab a notepad and pencil. "What's the assignment, Mrs. Flores?" he asked.

When AEGIS came calling, Jack was all business. It was one of the qualities that had rekindled Doc's affection for him three years ago. He could be the most hilarious joker in the room, but when danger reared its head, there was no better person to lead the charge against it.

Lucia reached into her clutch, producing a telegram and handing it to Doc. "We received this from West Orange at 3 p.m."

Unfolding the sheet of yellow paper in her hand, Doc scanned the text. It was the standard encryption used on all AEGIS communications. A hand-scrawled translation below each line deciphered the message into plain English.

The bureau chief cleared her throat. "A Norwegian merchant vessel, the *HDMS Lougen*, went missing in the Arctic in the late 1840s. The crew were presumed lost, although some Inuit hunters relayed tales of the ship being locked in the ice off the northern Greenland coast."

Jack scribbled notes on his pad, while Doc frowned at the telegram.

"But what's this about a radio signal?" she puzzled.

Jack blinked. "Radio signal?"

Lucia nodded. "A little over a week ago, we picked up a radio signal. Our regional listening posts were able to approximate its origin just off the—"

"Northern Greenland coast," Jack finished.

"Exactly where the local Inuit placed the *Lougen*," Lucia added.

Doc's brow furrowed, the same way it did every time the gears in her mind were hard at work. "Coincidence?"

"Absolutely possible," Lucia sighed, "but unlikely, given how much nothing is out there."

"What about this radio signal?" Jack asked. "What is it, exactly?"

Lucia shifted her round hips and leaned a hand on the heavy desk. "AEGIS Intelligence isn't sure. It began as a thirty-minute wave pattern, repeating every four hours for the first day, then it switched to a much shorter signal."

Jack frowned. "Still repeating?"

"Every four hours, for the past eight days," Lucia nodded.

"So why us?" Jack mused. "There must be a team in the arctic region who can investigate..."

Lucia looked around conspiratorially, then leaned over the desk. "Colonel Shaw requested your crew specifically," she explained, a look of absolute gravity on her face. "Apparently, a scientist at the British Secret Intelligence Service thought you should spearhead the investigation."

Jack and Doc exchanged a look.

"What scientist?" asked Doc.

Lucia produced a small notepad from her clutch and flipped it open. "Doctor Nariaal? Does that mean anything to you?"

Doc's eyes widened and she tossed the telegram to the desk, beginning to pace nervously. She remembered their last mission to engage the Silver Star at Noble's Isle in the

South Pacific, a place the native inhabitants called Sanctuary. The peculiar thing about the island was that it was largely populated by the descendants of a mad scientist's experiments with vivisection and animal-human grafting. Among their leaders had been a gorilla with a genius-level intelligence.

Nariaal.

He'd helped the combined crews of the *Daedalus*, *Percival*, and the *Nautilus*—an electric submarine commanded by the granddaughter of the infamous Captain Nemo—to fight off the occupation of the Silver Star.

In the aftermath, he'd decided to visit the outside world, having learned all he could on the island. Ultimately, he'd been given multiple post-graduate degrees from Cambridge University, and a position within the SIS, studying some secret technology that Britain had possessed since the 1890s.

"If Nariaal wants us on this," Jack said, "it means he thinks the signal might be..."

"Of extraterrestrial origin," Doc sighed.

Lucia's eyes bulged in their sockets.

Jack closed his notepad and tapped the pencil against its outside edge. "We'll need the crew called up."

Doc continued her pacing. "Last I heard, Ace was going through AEGIS officer training. I think he's currently assigned to the *Achilles*."

"That's correct," Lucia confirmed. "But we've already contacted the others. They'll rendezvous in West Orange." She pushed away from the desk. Administration was her wheelhouse. "Orders are to investigate the source of the signal, and retrieve it if possible. We've arranged air transport for you. The plane will be on your landing strip tomorrow morning at 0800."

"Not a lot of prep time," Doc muttered, her brain clicking away like a court stenographer's keypad.

Jack nodded. "We've got our usual gear ready to go. Everything else we can requisition from headquarters."

"Pack warm," Lucia warned, and then the phone rang.

All three stared at the candlestick device momentarily, caught off-guard by the sudden jangle.

Jack grabbed the phone, plucking the earpiece from its cradle and holding it to his ear. "McGraw," he announced. There was a brief burst of animated static as the voice on the other end spouted what sounded like a warning or alarm. Jack's face hardened into a concrete mask of determination. "Okay, Leo. Lock everything down. Be with you in a minute." He slammed the earpiece into the cradle and put the phone down with authority.

Doc blinked. "What is it, Jack?"

But Jack was already heading for the study doors. "We need to go. Now."

Wings heard the urgent footsteps down the main hallway and intercepted Jack as he went to an enormous painted portrait of the family hanging on the wall near its terminus. Ellen followed, eyes wide and curious.

"Leo spotted some suspicious activity out in the canyon, near the property line," Jack explained, opening the painting like a cabinet door. Inside was a metal safe with a key lock. Fishing his key ring from his pocket, he located the correct one and inserted it, twisting to open the heavy door. "It might be nothing," he added.

They heard the first shot, followed by a half dozen more.

"It's not nothing," Wings confirmed.

Reaching into the safe, Jack produced a canvas web belt with a holster secured to each side. He wrapped it around his waist and clipped it together in front. "Wings, you wanna pitch in some air support?"

The blond aviatrix grinned. "Hot damn! You know I do!"

Doc reached past Jack and pulled a Winchester carbine from the wall safe. Levering open the mechanism to find it empty, she began loading rounds from an open ammo box. "Who's on duty, aside from Leo?"

"Chin, I think. Severin and Costa are supposed to rotate on tomorrow." Jack unholstered a nickel-plated Colt automatic and checked the slide, then repeated the action with the matching pistol in the second holster. Both had fresh magazines. He knelt down to bring himself to eye level with Ellen, taking her shoulders in his large hands. "I need you to do me a big favor and help mommy hold down the fort, okay?"

Ellen's gaze found Jack's, and she nodded as he kissed her forehead. "I will."

As Jack rose, Wings was already out the back door. He leaned in to kiss Doc. "Douse the lights, and stay safe." He noticed Lucia had already conjured a .38 revolver from somewhere on her person. "Might want to get on the horn, call in some reinforcements, if this is what I think it is."

"What do you think it is, Captain McGraw?"

Jack tensed. "It's not a surprise the Silver Star know where we live." He descended the steps to the family room. "But this is a direct assault on our home. It's pretty brazen, and might indicate we're onto something they don't want us involved with."

Then Jack was out the back door, and Doc stood in the hall, ratcheting the last of the cartridges into the Winchester.

"The radio signal," she muttered quietly.

"Do you have another telephone?" Lucia asked, flicking the cylinder of the pistol open to check it.

"In the kitchen," Doc nodded. "Help yourself."

As Lucia stepped from the room, Doc and Ellen were left standing alone in the hall, overlooking the sunken family room and the rear of the house. The sound of gunfire erupted again from outside. Ellen hugged her arms around Doc's waist.

"Don't worry," the girl said. "Daddy will be okay."

Doc smiled at her daughter's optimism. "He always has been," she answered. "So far."

CR

The facade of the St. James hotel stood stark and regal against the dark Parisian sky, a stately monolith in the Porte Dauphine district. Its weathered neoclassical architecture hinted at unabashed luxury, sumptuous food and drink, a host of vices indulged in by the patrons within its walls. The fountain at the center of the circular drive vaulted jets of water which danced over electric lights, a shimmering, dazzling show for visitors and passersby.

The lobby was black-accented white marble and crushed red velvet, the stairway banisters English oak. The walls of the guest wing hallways were black, a long crimson carpet runner tracing the length of each spur.

Behind the heavy double doors to the executive suite was a deceptively vast apartment, furnished with French antiques, classical portraits adorning the walls, and a fire ablaze in the hearth.

A man slouched in the overstuffed armchair facing the fireplace, brown eyes blinking the cobwebs from his vision. An empty hypodermic needle sat in an ornately-carved pewter tray, next to the darkened cooking spoon and an opened paper ball that leaked grains of heroin onto the side table. The man was jowly, out of shape even for his 53 years.

His egg-shaped, bald head was surrounded by a fringe of hair that seemed to grow whiter by the month, and a gold and red silk robe hung loosely around his pale, flabby frame. He flexed his left hand, squeezing it into a fist several times as the feeling returned in a familiar prickly sensation. Pain at the injection site still radiated from his armpit, and he dabbed at the soreness with a handkerchief from the table.

Soft footsteps on carpet padded into the room from the makeshift office next door. The younger man was slender, blond, and dressed in a charcoal gray double-breasted suit. He carried a tray with a decanter of brandy and a small glass. "Master?" came the gentle query. "The Los Angeles...er, operation...is underway."

Aleister Crowley blinked again, becoming ever more aware of his surroundings. "Excellent," he grunted. He folded the spot of blood to the center of the hanky and set it aside. "Meantime, I have meditated on the source of the signal, and am convinced that it is of Elder origin."

"Astonishing, Master."

"We need to retrieve the object. It is of singular import."

The assistant bowed. "Yes, Master. Should we send the *Luftpanzer*?"

Crowley grunted. "The *Luftpanzer* is being refitted in Argentina, and Captain Ecke is nearing the end of his usefulness."

"Yes, Master. Has there been any word from Commander Blutig?"

The assistant traded the rectangular tray of heroin paraphernalia for the brandy, removing the stopper and pouring a small amount into the glass from the decanter.

Crowley plucked the cup from the table and sipped from it without looking at the man. Amber light from the hearth played across his bloated features, creating a frightening mask of megalomania.

His baggy, sunken eyes squinted for a long moment into the flames. Then: "Maria is gone. I find no hint of her whereabouts in any adjacent dimension. She is of no use here." He threw back the rest of the glass in a single gulp and returned it to the tray. "Dispatch Captain Hummel and the *Osiris* to claim our prize."

- CHAPTER 3 -

Jack hit the path running and found Jinx exiting the barn. The young man's worried expression told Jack that he was aware of something amiss.

"Somebody's shooting!" Jinx reported.

Jack grabbed his shoulder to turn him around, and they headed back to the barn at a brisk pace. "It's okay, Jinx. Leo and I will get this sorted out. Is the Harley running?"

"Purrs like a mama lion."

Jack pulled the right barn door open wide enough for two people to stand side-by-side, and beckoned Jinx into the massive building. "Okay, good. Now, son, I want you to stay put in here. Find a nice corner to wait this out, maybe over by the workbench, and hold tight until someone comes to fetch you back to the house. It's dangerous out there right now." He flicked on only one of the four work lights from a set of switches near the door.

"If it's bad guys, I can fight 'em!"

A bright smile broke across Jack's face. "I know you can, Jinx. You're a tough kid. But you're my best and only mechanic, and I don't want you taking a bullet by accident."

Jinx maintained his look of concern. Jack wasn't only his employer, he was his hero. He knew Jack would never lead him astray, or play a mean-spirited prank, like some of the crew did on the movie sets.

"Please," Jack urged again.

"Aye aye, Captain," Jinx saluted, disappearing toward the half-dozen engines in various states of assembly by a cluttered L-shaped workbench near the center of the barn.

Jack went directly to his preferred mode of ground transportation: the 1927 Harley Davidson JD he'd purchased upon returning from their last mission. He was a fan of the sleek, modern design, the low profile and elongated chassis, its superior power and handling. A teardrop gas tank swept back from beneath long handlebars, pointing toward a spring-reinforced, padded leather saddle. Its stock olive-green paint job gleamed in the barn's dim work light.

He'd ridden one in pursuit of Silver Star agents in the New York countryside a couple of years ago, and another one to flee Silver Star agents in the back alleys of Piraeus, Greece, just last year. He could say without any sense of hyperbole that those two machines had saved his life. Doc's, too. So when he found himself settling down on acreage in the hills of Southern California, this was the bike he chose to own.

He could hear the stuttered start of a far-off airplane engine, and knew Wings would be in the air in under a minute. Pulling the riding goggles from the handlebars, he quietly pushed the Harley through the gap in the barn doors. Once clear, he hauled the right door shut, standing illuminated by the lone exterior light at the center-most gable as he slipped the goggles onto his head.

Jack threw his right leg across the saddle, straddling the Harley and kicking down on the starter. Jinx wasn't wrong—the engine growled to life like a wild predator, roaring and snarling as he twisted the throttle. He leaned forward, forcing the kickstand up, shifting into gear with his left hand, and opened the throttle with his right.

As the Harley took off across the ranch, Jack watched Wanda Jensen's Curtiss plane rise into the evening sky. Its silhouette was black against the gunmetal blue and retreating purple backdrop of the last minutes of sunset. Night flying would be a bit of a challenge in the canyon, but Jack trusted her considerable skill in the cockpit. She'd gained a reputation as a barnstormer long before venturing to Los Angeles to work in pictures, and before getting drafted into the AEGIS organization.

The last of the summer breezes ruffled Jack's hair and shirt as he aimed the motorcycle toward the southwest telephone shack, where Leo Unger was stationed. Because of Jack and Doc's comparatively high profile, AEGIS paid for six loyal and dedicated security personnel for the ranch, two on duty at any given time.

Each telephone shack was ostensibly a bunkhouse with a heavy cot, weapons locker, and small office space, which included a desk, shortwave radio, observation windows, and a direct telephone line to the main house.

As Jack neared the structure, he noticed the lights were completely dark, inside and out. A Model T pickup truck sat, unoccupied and silent, on the north side. He braked to a halt and raised the motor goggles onto his forehead as Leo jogged around the back side of the truck to meet him, clutching a shotgun in his left hand.

Leo Unger, a former infantryman with the 369th New York, had forged a distinguished career, both at the Western Front and as a middleweight boxer and bodyguard. Now pushing fifty, he made his living as the head of security for the Starr-McGraw ranch. He was a wiry man of average stature, but projected a large personality. Ebony hair, clippered short, receded back to his bronze temples, a gray twill ivy cap covering his balding pate. His work shirt was open at the collar, mostly hidden beneath a brown leather jacket.

"What's your status?" Jack demanded.

"Got us a sniper on the ridge above the canyon trail," said Leo, his thin mustache undulating as he spoke. "Chin's working her way around behind."

Jack frowned. If agent Sarah Chin was at this end of the property, that left no one at the southeast telephone shack. "Show me."

Leo flattened against the east-facing outer wall of the shack, edging toward the corner. Jack followed, slowly rolling the rumbling cycle forward. Leo raised the shotgun to his shoulder and took aim at a copse of scrub brush along a rock shelf on the hillside.

There was a loud *crack*, and Jack saw the answering muzzle flash in the dark. The enemy shot flew wide, kicking dust and gravel from the path several feet to their left. But now Jack had a good idea where the assailant was.

"Cover me," he said. "I'm gonna draw his fire."

"Yessir!"

"And get ready to roll in the truck. This may be a diversion for a larger attack."

Jack opened the throttle to full, sending a rooster tail of dust behind his rear tire as the Harley screamed away into the dark. He expected to face a surgical tempest of sniper fire, but to his surprise, not a single shot came his way. The Harley bounced over divots and rocks, nosing down into the gully that ran east-west along the southern property line. Jack twisted the throttle, and the bike shot up the hill beyond, climbing toward the outcropping and the sniper's position.

The scrub brush jostled with movement within. Jack braked to a gravelly halt, throttling to idle and standing from the saddle. Grabbing a pistol from its holster with his right hand, he aimed the headlamp on the front fork into the bushes along with the Colt. "Come on out!" he ordered. "We've got you surrounded! There's no escape!"

A feminine voice answered his challenge. "It's Agent Chin, Captain! I got the sniper!" The young woman stood from the tangle of weeds and brush, bloody hunting knife in a sturdy right hand. She wasn't much more than five-foot-two, slender and pale, with her hair in a ponytail. Gray jodhpurs and a black leather jacket blended into the surrounding darkness like intentional camouflage.

Her father, Henry Chin, was one of a handful of Chinese-Americans to serve in the Great War, part of the Lost Battalion slaughtered in the Argonne forest. She'd taken his loss hard, channeling her rage toward something positive, joining the AEGIS Security Division under the sponsorship of San Francisco private detective Danny Long.

As she squinted in the glare of the motorcycle headlight, several tendrils of wispy, black, acrid smoke began to stretch up from the body at her feet. She glanced down, aghast at the sight of the dead man in the black uniform as he dissolved away to a pile of dust and bone shards.

That answered that question. The *Astrum Argentum* knew where Jack and his family lived, and they were probing his defenses.

"Good work, Sarah," Jack nodded, turning the front of the cycle back to face east. "They do that." He referred to the dissolving body of the Silver Star agent, a failsafe against capture.

In the distance, the sound of a gunshot echoed across the canyon trailheads. Jack gazed east toward the noise. "Meet up with Leo and follow me in the truck."

Jack had been fighting the minions of Aleister Crowley for the past three years, and had yet to be surprised by their tactics. They could pop up anytime, anywhere, but once they were engaged, they fought in a very paint-by-numbers manner. Jack theorized that it was probably due to Crowley not having a mind for military tactics, as well as possessing little in the way of basic regard for human life beyond his own. He played at being a general as a child might move toy soldiers around a playroom floor. A child with a virtually unlimited supply of expendable figurines.

This was a classic Silver Star attack.

He snapped the goggles back over his eyes. Revving the Harley, he roared down the incline, into the gully, and out the other side. The bike leaped into the air, coming down with a lurch on the dusty path. Jack could hear the Ford's engine behind him—Leo and Sarah would be along presently.

The roar of Wings and her Curtiss bellowed overhead as the biplane strafed the southern property line, leaving a trail of white phosphorus flares that bounced along the ground before lying still.

The motorcycle's headlamp flooded the distance ahead, illuminating the southeast portion of the property along with the flares. Several dark shapes moved from the cover of the trailhead into the orchard. Foregoing the gear shifter, Jack took aim with his left hand and fired the Colt across the handlebars. Squeezing the trigger repeatedly, he emptied the magazine. Two agents fell near the first line of trees, but most of his shots were off-mark.

The Curtiss banked hard and climbed to make another pass. Like Jack's new bird, it wasn't armed, but he knew Wings kept a stash of personal munitions aboard, and had even been known to target shoot with small arms from the cockpit. Now that she'd helped illuminate the property with her flares, she'd start paying special attention to the men on the ground.

Submachine guns chattered from deeper within the walnut grove, sending hot hornets of lead buzzing past the motorcycle. Jack shoved the empty Colt back into its holster. He was tempted to reach across his waist for its twin, but decided to keep both hands on the bars, weaving the bike left and right in a simple evasive maneuver. He needed to close with the enemy agents. Guns barked, bullets whizzing by his head.

Just as the pickup truck caught up to him, its lights fell across a swath of ground in front of him. A small cylindrical object skittered ahead of the Harley's front fork. Eyes suddenly wide, Jack leaned over left, putting the bike chassis between himself and the exploding stick grenade.

A blinding flash and explosive roar accompanied the sulfurous smoke, as gravel and metal shards shredded the Harley's undercarriage and tore open the radiator on the pickup. The motorcycle flipped side-over-side, but Jack kicked free as it did, rolling parallel to it. Even so, the front fork impacted his left shoulder and he grunted in agony as it wrenched out of its socket.

A second explosion lifted the pickup truck a foot in the air and dumped it on its side, windows shattered, a small fire igniting under the engine compartment.

Jack groaned, flailing in an effort to sit upright but only able to scoot along the dirt path, left arm limp and devoid of feeling. He watched as the Curtiss did a backward wingover and nosed down toward the orchard, shots ringing out from the pistol in the pilot's hand.

If Jack was going to check on Leo and Sarah before the fire spread to the gas tank, it would have to be now, while Wings was running interference.

The diving plane traded gunfire with the agents in the walnut grove. Another flare lit up the orchard from the ground.

Staggering to a vaguely upright position, left arm hanging at his side, Jack trudged to the overturned Ford and peered through the shattered windscreen. Frustrated, he tore the goggles from his head with his good hand.

Leo lay crumpled against the passenger side door, unconscious.

Jack stumbled around the truck's front end to the rear window of the cab. He was pretty sure he could get Leo out through that, if he could get his shoulder back in place. Scanning around the trailside, he saw the slumped form of Sarah Chin about twenty feet away from the truck bed. She'd either been thrown clear when the truck flipped, or in the midst of a hasty exit, and knocked down in the explosion.

Order of operations, he thought. *Shoulder, Leo, Sarah.*

Facing the sideways cab of the pickup, Jack clenched his jaw and leaned his loose arm against its steel roof. Then he threw his entire weight forward, forcing the ball of his shoulder back into its socket. A sobering wave of pain washed over him, and he screamed through gritted teeth. Feeling returned to his arm in waves of pinpoints.

Scrunching his hand repeatedly into a fist to accelerate recovery, he yanked the right pistol from its holster and smashed the Ford's back window. He ran the barrel of the nickel-plated Colt around the frame, clearing the broken shards of glass before replacing the pistol at his hip.

The fire was spreading from the engine compartment, smoke beginning to pour into the cab.

There was no good way to do this. He was making an executive decision and risking possible further damage to Leo's spine in order to save him from burning. If he was even still alive.

Crouching slightly to get a better grip on the man's jacket, he hauled Leo headfirst through the back window, dragging the unconscious body to a spot next to the motionless form of Sarah Chin. Jack knelt over Leo, checking for a pulse, then doing the same for Sarah.

They were both alive, but Leo was bleeding from the nose and ears, and Sarah had a pretty considerable bump on the forehead. They both needed medical attention, sooner rather than later.

He glanced up to see the Curtiss as it swooped and dove over the orchard, engaging with the remaining Silver Star agents in the trees. Then something heavy clubbed him in the ribs, sending Jack sprawling to the dirt as the agent hefted the heavy stock of the MP-18 in giant, calloused hands.

Momentarily dazed, Jack fumbled absentmindedly for the loaded Colt in his right holster, but found it inaccessible underneath him.

The Silver Star agent was a large Romanian in black commando fatigues and a billed service cap. He lowered the barrel of the submachine gun and squeezed the trigger, eliciting a suspicious click from within the gun.

Jack stared at the agent, who stared back at Jack. Then Jack rolled off his right leg, freeing the holster with the loaded .45.

As Jack's hands scratched at dirt and canvas to undo the snap, the agent tossed the MP-18 aside, replacing it with a wicked-looking combat blade from his left boot.

Jack's right hand thrust out, clutching the Colt, which the agent immediately kicked away. The man stood over Jack's shuddering form, taking in his shock and visceral terror as he tried to find purchase to stand. As he did, the agent lunged, and although Jack did his best to parry, the blade parted the flesh of his right leg.

A punch to the agent's solar plexus knocked him back a couple feet, and the knife came along with his hand. The agent whirled around in some kind of spinning kick, and once again Jack collapsed to the ground, head ringing with the unexpected blow. He rolled onto his back, scuttling slowly away from his attacker on skinned hands. He watched as the agent tossed the knife from right hand to left, then back again.

The blade glistened, already slick with his blood, in the light of the flares. The entire attack had caught him off-guard. The agent was as big as he was, and had the advantage of a weapon. He didn't know how he was going to get out of this.

The heavy crack of a nearby gunshot pierced the evening air. The agent's head snapped back, then rolled forward. He sank to his knees, his face a blank mask of shock. Blood coursed down his face from the entry wound in his forehead, and he crumpled to the dusty ground.

Jack looked up and saw Bill Hart astride his brown and white pinto, Fritz. The silver glint of a long-barreled revolver shone from his right hand as the horse reared in place. "Heard the shots and thought you might need some help before the law showed up," he drawled.

A distant wail of sirens approaching from deeper in Santa Clarita up Newhall Avenue hung in the air.

Jack grunted and groaned as he staggered to his feet, and Hart swung his leg over the saddle, dismounting with a flourish.

"Much obliged," Jack smiled, adding, "partner" for good measure.

Bill Hart would have returned a smile at the sentiment, had he not been transfixed at the sight of the fallen agent consumed in black smoke, withering away to a pile of desiccated, dusty remains. "Holy—"

"Yeah, they do that," Jack said for the second time that night.

"I've seen the serials," Hart marveled, "but I guess I didn't think..."

Jack chuckled low in his throat. "That it's real?" He stooped to pick up the loaded Colt from a few paces away, listening to the approaching sirens and the occasional *pop-pop-pop* of small arms fire as Wings continued to strafe the remaining agents in the orchard. "Bill, let me tell you...I've seen things. Glad you decided to drop by."

"Just being neighborly," Hart replied, pushing the brim of his Stetson high on his forehead. "Though I'd appreciate it if you'd keep your little girl from buzzing my place..."

"Done and done," Jack chuckled. "We're gonna be taking a little family trip anyway. Dunno how long we'll be gone."

"Dare I ask?"

"AEGIS business."

"Ah," Hart nodded. "'Nuff said."

Two police sedans, flanked by a couple of motorcycle cops and followed by an ambulance, pulled off the front drive and onto the path toward the canyon trailhead. Jack watched as Doc emerged from the back of the house, followed by Ellen and Lucia.

Jinx appeared from the barn, ambling hesitantly toward the burning truck. Bill Hart waved his cowboy hat to signal the ambulance over to their location.

Jack scanned the property and noted the gunfire from the orchard had ceased. Either Wings had eliminated the rest of the agents, or they'd been frightened off. Jack made a mental bet on the former. He knew a search would yield nothing but some shredded uniforms and small piles of bone and ash.

How many had been in the attacking force was unknown, but they'd been able to hold the fort with two security guards, a stunt pilot, a Western movie star, and an aging war hero on a motorcycle.

Is that the best you can do, Crowley? he thought. *You just come on ahead and give us your best shot. We'll send you packing. Again.*

- CHAPTER 4 -

Between the police presence, the search for any remaining Silver Star agents on the property, putting out literal fires, and packing mission essentials, no one got much sleep. Jinx wandered the property with a water canister on his back, spraying various small blazes with a pressurized wand.

Leo Unger and Sarah Chin were taken to LA County Hospital for observation and treatment, expected to fully recover. When medics offered to see to Jack's bleeding leg and various abrasions, Doc protectively declined, insisting on tending his wounds herself. She'd been digging bullets out of this man and stitching him up for the past three years, not including their time in the war. She damn well knew the business of Jack McGraw's healing and recovery better than any stranger at County.

Bill Hart returned to Horseshoe Ranch about midnight, and the last of the cops departed at 2 a.m., after some new AEGIS security personnel came on duty.

Finally satisfied the ranch was secure, Lucia Flores drove away at 3:45. Wings fell asleep on the living room sofa, snoring with Ellen's unconscious head rising and falling on her chest. In reality, Wanda Jensen was effectively itinerant, so she was the first to volunteer her services as a house sitter while the family was away.

With clothing and personal gear stowed and sitting ready for the plane, wounds sutured and properly dressed, Jack and Doc finally collapsed into each other's arms on the master bed at 5:15 a.m.

When Wings entered the bedroom to roust them at 7:30, she made sure to do it with a mug of hot coffee in each hand. Jack managed a quick shave and sponge bath before shrugging into a clean gray twill traveling suit and matching fedora. Doc opted for a simple floral-print skirt and white silk top, with a short taupe fall jacket and cloche hat.

By the time they descended to the main floor, they could already hear the Ford trimotor airplane outside. Ellen sat in the breakfast nook between the kitchen and family room, sucking down a small glass of orange juice. Wings had already helped her dress in a sailor top, white shorts, and black leather Mary Janes. Her strawberry waves were pulled back from her face with a pair of decorative butterfly hair clips.

"If you need anything while we're away," Doc instructed Wings, "don't hesitate to call Mr. Hart. And of course Lucia Flores."

"Don't worry," Wings sighed. "I've got your six."

"Thanks, Wanda," Doc smiled.

Jack gulped down his cup of coffee. "Yes, indeedy. Thanks, Wings."

Ellen slid out of the nook and went down the short staircase, through the sunken family room, to the back door, where she picked up her leather travel pack and slid it over a tired shoulder. "Hey, let's go," she urged. She clearly could not wait to get back in the air, even as a passenger on a commercial aircraft.

Jack and Doc ambled out back to the landing strip, each clutching a duffel bag and a backpack of crucial gear. Ellen passed them and ended up leading the way. Wings brought up the rear, carrying a small suitcase that Ellen had forgotten.

Jinx was nowhere to be seen, but then he hadn't gone to bed until nearly dawn. Wings promised she'd extend their goodbyes.

Jack whistled in appreciation as they approached the gravel landing strip. The trimotor was an incredible machine, painted a flat gray with the AEGIS winged shield and sword insignia on the sides and tail. It was of all-metal construction, with a 74-foot wingspan and corrugated surfaces. One propeller idled at the aircraft's broad nose, with another slung under each massive wing. A two-person cockpit with the most modern instrumentation sat back from the nose prop, above a luxury passenger compartment that seated seven.

The passenger door stood open, monitored by a tall Swedish woman in a blue double-breasted skirt suit and matching beret. A dark-haired pilot in a button-down shirt and tie, wearing the same jodhpurs and knee boots favored by Jack and Doc, made a visual inspection of the outside as the family embarked. He unlocked a hatch at the rear for the luggage.

"Hallo," the attendant greeted. "I am Astrid. Please leave your luggage right here, and Mr. Martin will load it before we take off."

Ellen didn't need to be told twice. She dropped her pack and climbed into the flying parlor, strapping into her seat in ten seconds flat.

Jack pushed the brim of his fedora up on his forehead. "If it's all the same to you, ma'am, we'd like to keep an eye on our gear."

Doc, Wings, and Jack hauled the bags to the rear cargo area and began handing them to the pilot, but were interrupted by the man's effusive welcome. He smiled, shaking their hands excitedly in turn.

"Captain Stratosphere!" the pilot beamed.

Jack smiled politely, wincing inside. While he was generally accepting of the nickname during the war, and for his own use in public relations, hearing other people address him formally with it still caused some discomfort. He wasn't sure why. Perhaps because he'd never actually gone to the stratosphere.

"Cal Martin," the man introduced, pumping his hand with gusto. "I've heard so much about your exploits for AEGIS!"

Jack nodded as politely as he could with the lack of sleep. "Pleased to meet you, Cal. This is Doc, and Wings."

"Doctor Starr, Miss Jensen."

Jack handed the first of the duffel bags to the grinning man, and he finally got the point. Doc stepped away to the passenger door and entered the plane, while Jack kept Cal occupied with baggage and conversation.

"This a 4-AT?" Jack asked.

"4-AT-E, actually."

"It's got the double cockpit?"

"Yessir. Doris is already at the helm!"

"How long do we expect to New Jersey?"

"With five fuel stops and some rest breaks, we're going to try to get you there in about two days."

Jack pursed his lips, impressed. Commercial air travel had sure evolved in the years since the end of the war. He handed Cal the last bag and patted the pilot on the shoulder. "Well, we're probably gonna sleep the first leg. You might've heard we had a rather late night."

Cal nodded solemnly. "Yes, we heard. Silver Star agents attacked your home?!"

"They tried," Jack winked, stepping toward the passenger door. The blond attendant gestured to the folding steps below the portal.

"Give 'em hell, Jack!" Wings saluted from the tarmac.

Jack turned, hunched over in the doorway. "Make sure Jinx gets enough to eat. And no parties with your movie industry friends!" Chuckling at his joke—because Wings had no movie industry friends—he disappeared within.

Cal fastened the latch on the cargo door and stepped into the plane, followed by Astrid, who pulled the ladder up to its fold-away position and closed the hatch behind her.

Ellen waved at Wings from her seat next to a forward window.

Doc settled into a plush chair behind Ellen, Jack taking his seat opposite. Astrid made sure their safety belts were fastened, then moved forward to the crew compartment, disappearing behind a slate gray curtain.

By the time the trimotor was in the air, all three passengers were sound asleep again.

Their first stop for refueling was about four hours later in St. George, Utah. The next leg would be a nearly five-hour trek across the Rockies to Denver. Astrid brought them cold box lunches and soda pop, and halfway through the journey, they watched the silent epic adventure *The Lost World*, starring Wallace Beery.

Doc was amazed they'd outfitted the plane with a movie projector and screen, but was informed the practice was common among commercial carriers on longer flights.

Ellen liked the animated dinosaurs, and her eyes widened in wonder when Jack told her it was based on a real expedition to the Maple White plateau in South America.

They ran into some foul weather two hours outside Omaha. The storm tossed the plane around like a baseball in a game of catch, the end result being that everyone was quite sick by the time they landed. They disembarked and slept in the pilot quarters at the airfield, aloft again at first light.

The plane refueled a fourth time in Chicago. Its fifth and final stop was in Pittsburgh, then straight on to Kenilworth, New Jersey. Doc nudged Jack awake as they descended over the airfield he once called home. He'd first encountered the giant airship *Luftpanzer* in the skies over this place, engaging Silver Star fighter pilots without armaments of his own. Just moments after landing, Doc had reappeared in his life after a seven-year absence, and kick-started their whole new life together.

Only three years ago, Kenilworth had been a sleepy rural airstrip with a single hangar and a few outbuildings. It had been the headquarters of Jack's employer, Morton Aviation. After the death of James Morton at the hands of Silver Star agents, Thomas Edison had purchased Morton's share of stock in the company, its assets rolled into the greater AEGIS effort. That effort was now a massive international research and paramilitary organization.

Doris Dalton, Cal's co-pilot, was first to disembark, followed by Astrid, who assisted her sore and creaky-legged passengers to the solid ground outside. A statuesque brunette, Doris opened the cargo hold and began to offload the duffel bags, as Jack took a moment to scan the facility from the end of the landing strip.

Much had changed in three years: the single hangar was now a six-plane affair, with a full shop and administrative offices attached. A control tower stood proudly where the old pilots' bunkhouse used to be, and there was now a small community of bungalows surrounding the airfield, able to accommodate a full staff complement and their families. But perhaps the most drastic change was the presence of two mammoth aerodromes, giant airship hangars 960 feet in length, 320 feet wide and almost 200 feet high.

"You're drooling," Doc chuckled, handing him his canvas bag with a grunt.

"Darn right I'm drooling," Jack replied, suddenly intent on a tour.

Ellen noticed a familiar form approaching from the control tower and her eyes grew to the size of saucers. "Uncle Charlie!"

Jack and Doc both turned, identical smiles breaking across each of their faces.

Charlie Dalton was of Cherokee extraction, a wiry man in his thirties, with a well-tanned olive complexion and raven black hair in a clippered fade. As he approached, Doc noticed he was wearing the uniform and rank pips of a Lieutenant Commander in the AEGIS Special Operations division. It wasn't entirely different from the US Army doughboy uniform he'd been wearing pieces of ever since the war: buff khaki trousers and snap-on puttees, a matching cotton work shirt, and a brown leather jacket with various patches denoting division and duty assignment. A crimson beret bearing the AEGIS insignia was cocked at an angle atop his head.

A decorated veteran of the Great War, Dalton had been a code-talker, pathfinder, and sharpshooter, cool under fire and fearless of the most hazardous duty. For most of his career, he'd become known simply by the moniker "Deadeye".

"Good to see you, Red," he laughed as he swept Ellen up in a celebratory embrace.

Doc rushed to him, wrapping her arms around him and kissing his cheek as he set Ellen down. "Charlie!" she gushed. "You look great!"

"What's this?" Jack smirked as he approached his old comrade. He reached out, flicking the rank pips on Deadeye's jacket collar. "Lieutenant Commander?"

Charlie gave Jack's hand a strong shake, cracking a half-smile. "Yeah, they're just giving commissions away now," he said, soft baritone tinged with a slight Carolina drawl.

"How's the *Daedalus*?" Jack asked. "Have you seen her?"

"Just got in last night, actually. Been on assignment in Morocco with Kate."

Doc raised an eyebrow. "What's going on in Morocco?"

"Setting up a new field office, picking up the pieces from the last conflict with Spain, mostly."

Jack nodded, squinting. "How's it looking out there?"

Charlie's smile faded instantly. "It's a mess, Cap. Sometimes it feels like the war never ended."

"It only ended on paper," Doc agreed. "So where's Kate now?"

"Still in Morocco. I'll go back when we're finished in Greenland."

A Model T pickup rattled to a halt next to the plane, and a field technician in coveralls and a brimmed work cap jumped out, loading the luggage from the tarmac into the truck's open bed.

"Careful with that gear," Deadeye admonished. "They're in Bungalow C."

The worker gave a nod and a small salute, climbing back into the truck to drive it across the airfield to the residential area on the opposite side.

"Bungalow C?" Doc asked.

"They're nice," Deadeye's smile returned. "Comfy beds." He gestured after the pickup truck. "Shall we?"

Jack, Doc and Ellen said their farewells to Astrid and their pilots. It had been a marathon flight, but Doris and Cal had brought them through safely. The airplane crew remained to oversee its removal to the main hangar, and the passengers wandered away toward the bungalows with Deadeye.

Jack patted his inside jacket pocket for a pack of gum. "So when are we gonna—"

"See the ship?" Deadeye finished. "We'll go after lunch. Let's get y'all settled and changed first."

Their luggage was already inside when they reached Bungalow C. The residential units were as Charlie had described; comfortable, homey, and well-appointed. Theirs was a two-bedroom detached unit, with a single bathroom and a corner kitchenette. A wide, covered porch overlooked the airfield and all of its comings and goings.

Doc wasted no time in changing into her field outfit: dun-colored jodhpurs and brown leather knee boots, khaki work shirt with an open collar and red kerchief around her neck, almost ascot-like. Jack donned his navy blue uniform trousers with a gold stripe down the outside of each leg, black pilot boots, white cotton t-shirt, and a gray suede field jacket festooned with his AEGIS division and service patches.

Ellen swapped her sailor top and shorts for a white button-down shirt and a set of blue denim bib overalls. If they were going to the aerodrome, she couldn't very well be expected to wear her Sunday best.

After a light lunch of sandwiches and iced tea—served on the bungalow porch, which impressed Ellen to no end—Deadeye escorted the trio to the first of the twin aerodromes. They were massive free-standing constructs of steel and concrete, with a row of skylights set along each of their spines.

Gargantuan doors opened to the south in paneled sections, and a mix of vehicles and people went to and fro, engaged in various deliveries and technical objectives. The sounds of very smart people building things echoed throughout the cavernous hangar. Within, a complex beehive of catwalks and latticeworks surrounded the space, reserved for an airship to be maintained or repaired.

In this case, the real estate allotted for a new *Heracles* class of AEGIS supercarrier to rival the size and armaments of its Silver Star counterpart, the *Osiris*, was occupied by a ship less than one-third its proposed scale. The AEGIS airship *Daedalus* sat in a makeshift slip of steel and wood, her freshly-painted silvery skin glistening in columns of diffuse light from the windows above.

She was bullet-shaped, not quite 250 feet in length and 128 feet in width. The window panels of the bridge angled down under the nose, and four outboard engine pods protruded from the main body, just proud of the envelope. Her outermost layer was vulcanized canvas, reinforced with aluminum powder resin, so although lightweight, it was surprisingly resilient.

Her name was painted in large black letters on each side of the body, with her registry —LR3-1—just above the aft-most engines. Her bones were constructed of perforated aluminum and an experimental "foam steel", which had proved its worth in the ship's previous incarnation.

A narrow gondola section ran most of the belly, beginning at a ball turret set back from and beneath the bridge. A row of observation windows and a sliding entry door were set in each side. The aft section included the airfoil struts for two large Ford-built thruster engines, and a rear cargo access ramp.

Three large stabilizer fins sprouted from the rear, two lateral and one vertical. The edges of all three were painted with a crimson stripe, and the AEGIS winged shield emblem proudly proclaimed itself from the upright tailfin. A dorsal ball turret and safety rail running aft from the top hatch was hidden from the observers below.

Someone in standard-issue denim mechanic's coveralls descended from the open port-side gondola door, and Doc immediately recognized the bright smile that flashed across the woman's face.

"Sparks!" she hailed, rushing to meet the young engineer in an informal hug.

Dhakiya Kitur was slender but solidly-built, her raven hair knotted into intricate braids under a steel-blue cotton bandanna. Her eyes gleamed dark amber in the hazy light, her features angular and regal. She was Kenyan, of native Kikuyu ancestry, the orphaned daughter of a tribal chief. Her entire village had been slaughtered by Indian troops under the command of a corrupt British officer. Since signing on as the chief engineer aboard the *Daedalus*, she'd modified existing AEGIS dynamo technology, improving output by ten percent per generator, and eliminating the requirement to take them offline for winding. That spelled a major agency-wide uptick in efficiency.

"How are you, Doc?" Sparks grinned, legitimately happy to see them all. She exchanged hugs with Jack and Charlie. "Captain, Deadeye, you're looking good!" Then she spotted Ellen at her mother's hip, stopping down to scoop her into a tight embrace. "And Ellen! You're getting so big!"

The young girl flashed a toothsome grin. "Guess what, Sparks—my dad's been teaching me to fly!"

The mechanic laughed as she stood, leveling a sarcastic expression at Jack. "Oh good!"

"Don't worry," Jack offered with a smirk. "She won't have her pilot's license for at least another six months."

Sparks gave a throaty chuckle. "Heavens help us."

"Ship looks good," Deadeye observed.

Doc stuck her thumbs inside her belt. "What have you been working on?"

Sparks lit up with the opportunity for a small boast. "Well, you know how lift gases shrink in cold temperatures..."

"Like many things," Doc added.

Deadeye snorted, and Jack rolled his eyes. "Dunno what you're talking about."

"And not just the lift gas," Sparks continued, ignoring Doc's jab at male physiology. "Air density is greater as well, so overall buoyancy is diminished. Even though we're using the hydrogen-helium mixture, we stand to lose much lift in such a cold region. So I developed a heating system for the ballonets, to keep the envelope from collapsing and retain maximum lift."

"No danger of igniting the hydrogen?" Deadeye pondered.

Sparks shook her head. "Not as long as we keep the mixture at least ten percent helium. Anything under that, and we run some risks."

"Sounds reasonable," Jack muttered, folding his arms across his chest.

Doc glanced at her watch. "We should probably go check in with Mr. Edison."

"He's not here," Sparks replied. "He's already gone to Fort Myers."

Doc frowned. "Florida?"

"You know he's got that botanical lab down there," Jack said. "Been his winter home for a few years now."

"Yeah," Doc sighed. "Just disappointing not being able to say hello."

"AEGIS has grown beyond Edison," Deadeye observed. "There's a whole command structure now. It's a lot less makeshift than when we joined up." He scuffed his boot heel absentmindedly on the concrete floor. "Which is probably a good thing."

Doc raised an eyebrow, but wasn't sure she wanted to have that conversation right then.

"Come on," Jack nudged. "Let's check in at headquarters. Make sure everything's jake."

Sparks bent with her hands on her knees, giving Ellen a broad smile. "How would you like a tour of the *Daedalus*?"

"You don't mind?" Doc asked.

"Not at all. We'll be fine."

"Yippee!" Ellen cheered, and the two ambled away to the silver-white dirigible.

Jack gazed around the vast interior of the aerodrome, marveling at the machine this philanthropic organization had become. True, it wasn't like they'd ever been personal friends of everyone involved in the agency, but since its inception in 1920, it had grown to mammoth proportions, with field offices the world over, and intricate relationships with various world governments. It had its own paramilitary force, including an aero-navy and an all-female unit of rocket-pack commandos.

And now it was working with the British government on the development of new technology based on harvested Martian hardware from the secret invasion of 1894. There was talk of sending up a manned moon shot within the next decade.

AEGIS was truly on the move. But then so was the *Astrum Argentum*. To what degree, Jack could only guess. In fact, he had an ever-growing list of questions forming in his head, including what the reasoning was behind the assault on his and Doc's home in Los Angeles.

But as he fished a stick of chewing gum from his front shirt pocket, he had a hunch this mission might bring some answers to light.

- CHAPTER 5 -

It was no surprise that Edison was spending more and more time in Florida; the headquarters at Glenmont Manor was crowded with people and buzzing with activity. What had begun as a gathering of wealthy industrialists with a social conscience—something Doc quietly believed was an oxymoron—was now a fully autonomous endeavor. Jack had to agree that Deadeye was right: AEGIS had truly grown beyond its humble origins.

Men in long coats with AEGIS badges patrolled the entire property with rifles or Tommy guns slung over their shoulders. Lighter-than-air patrol craft circled high overhead. There was now a black wrought iron fence surrounding the estate, with a guarded checkpoint at the front gate.

A black Cadillac limousine dropped them at the covered entry, which was monitored by armed security officers in bowlers and three-piece suits. The former entry was now a lobby, with a front desk and a telephone switchboard.

A petite redhead in a blue uniform skirt and blazer with AEGIS Administration division patches signed them in. They were immediately ushered upstairs to one of the east-wing guest quarters, which had been converted to a conference room sometime within the past year.

Joe Salyer, a short, bespectacled man of middle age, stood beside a mahogany desk that was covered in file folders and colorful charts. He was wearing the same gray suit he'd been in when Jack and Doc had last seen him in Port-au-Prince three years ago.

Marissa Singh, a slim Indian woman in her late twenties, sat on a love seat of maroon velvet, perusing an open file folder marked *CONFIDENTIAL*. She wore the blue and gray uniform of the AEGIS Aviation division, with trousers and knee boots identical to Jack's. Her black hair was braided and pinned back in a bun under her red beret, the glint of a ruby *bindi* visible in the center of her tan forehead. Upon seeing the trio enter the room, she stood and swooped in to greet them.

"Captain! Doc! Deadeye!" she cried joyfully in her chirpy English accent, hugging them in turn.

Jack's face radiated a broad smile from ear to ear. "Cipher! Good to see you!"

"You look great!" Doc gushed.

Deadeye squinted at her jacket collar, pointing out some new rank pips. "Been making the most of your time back, I see," he drawled with a mild smirk.

Cipher glanced down briefly, then nodded toward his own jacket. "I see you've been up to no good as well," she joked, "my fellow *Leftenant Commander*."

"AEGIS is clearly grooming you for your own command," Doc observed.

Salyer cleared his throat. "If we could begin the briefing," he grumbled. "I do need to be in the city for a dinner engagement..."

"Yes, of course," said Jack, stepping forward to shake his hand. "Good to see you, Mr. Salyer."

"Good to have you all back with us." The itinerant administrator pulled a file from the top of the stack on the desk and began poring over it. "As you already know, our listening stations in the northern hemisphere have been picking up a radio signal emanating from a location in the Arctic, off the coast of Greenland. In the vicinity of a mercantile ship we think has been stuck out there in the ice for the past seventy-five, eighty years."

Jack wrung his hands together, cracking knuckles as he did so. "Has there been any change to the frequency or duration of the signals?"

Cipher cast a look at Salyer, who nodded back at her. She returned to the sofa and plucked a hand-drawn chart from where she'd been sitting. "No change. Every four hours, for the past...ten days now," she said, reading the data from the sheet of paper in her hands.

"Any better idea what it could be?" Doc asked.

Cipher took a deep breath, fixing Doc's gaze with her own. "I've listened to a recording of the signal myself, and it's like nothing I've ever heard before." She returned the chart to the pile of papers on the couch, folding her arms in front of her. "I'm convinced it's some form of code, because of the sound patterns and the way it repeats. But it's no code I'm familiar with, nor does the actual signal sound...terrestrial to me."

Doc's eyes grew wide. "Do you think...?"

Joe Salyer leaned back against the desk, hands thrust into his pants pockets. "Doctor Starr, you've been studying the inscriptions on the harvested Martian technology the British Secret Intelligence Service shared with us last summer. Perhaps you should have a listen to the recordings and formulate a theory on that."

"I'll do that," said Doc.

Cipher pressed her point. "The signal almost wasn't picked up in the first place, it's at such a low frequency. That's another reason I don't think it originates from human technology."

"A beacon, perhaps?" Jack posited, rubbing his jaw.

Doc nodded. "My thought exactly."

"Hold on," Deadeye huffed. "A beacon? From where? Calling who?"

"Calling *whom*," corrected Cipher.

Jack pursed his lips, frowning. "Could be anything. A Martian probe. Some ancient technology reawakened."

"We don't know yet," Doc protested. "Which is why we're going to investigate."

"One thing's for sure," noted Jack. "If it's not Silver Star technology, it's something Crowley is going to be interested in. If they're not already en route, they will be in short order."

"Agreed," Deadeye muttered. "We should be ready for a fight."

Salyer circled the desk, beginning to put papers back in folders and stack them in a single pile. "Time is of the essence, ladies and gentlemen. We've engaged a local Inuit guide who will rendezvous with you in Nuuk. Knows the north country. That's the file on top, there. We already have cold weather gear requisitioned for you. It will be loaded tonight. You depart at dawn." He leveled a serious glance at Jack. "Unless you can think of a reason not to."

Jack held up his hands at chest height in protest. "Not a one," he said. "If Sparks has the *Daedalus* in working order, I think we're ready to go."

Salyer nodded, pulling the glasses from his nose and folding them into his breast pocket. "Then Godspeed, *Daedalus* crew. Consider your mission underway. Check in when you reach Greenland."

Joe Salyer packed up his valise and exited the room, shaking hands as he left. The file folders were left for the crew to read over. Jack decided that the mission loadout should lean toward survival gear and munitions, as they would have a full six-person crew complement and had to worry about every ounce of excess weight in the freezing temperatures which awaited them. AEGIS tended to over-supply, allowing ship commanders to pare down the gear they took on board prior to departure.

Twenty or so minutes into the planning session, a messenger knocked on the door and announced that Doc had visitors in the lobby.

The four collected up their file folders and headed down to greet Doc's aunts, Agnes and Millicent. The party, which now numbered six, rode back to the Kenilworth facility in the limousine, reuniting with Sparks and Ellen.

They gathered at the commissary for a delicious hot dinner, and when they were done, Agnes and Millie took charge of their grandniece. Their passage was already booked on the *SS California* to Glasgow, departing early the following day, and they had a room at the St. Charles Hotel for the night. Jack and Doc would reconnect with them in Edinburgh after the mission.

There were tears and tight embraces as Ellen bid farewell to her mother and father, but losing them on a dangerous mission never once entered her mind. Her parents serving the greater good on some perilous assignment was all she'd ever known. When they were together, they spent every hour of respite as a loving, nurturing family. Even when they weren't around, they made sure her needs were met. So how could she begrudge them a few weeks or even months away when it was in the service of order and civilization and all that was good in the world?

Ellen watched from the back of the limousine as the dual aerodrome shrank into the night. She yawned, imagining the daring adventures she might have someday.

With the loadout underway, Jack and Doc managed about four hours sleep between them. They reported before dawn at the aerodrome to find the *Daedalus* had been equipped with a full stock of food rations, potable water, and ammunition for the two gun turrets.

As the sun dared peek above the eastern horizon, a dozen AEGIS Aviation division ground crew guided the small airship forward through the giant hangar door, cleating her to the tarmac with aluminum cables. Deadeye stood a safe distance away, duffel bag at the ready, his two favorite rifles slung over his shoulder.

"You waiting for an engraved invitation?" Jack chuckled as he passed Charlie, clapping a hand on his back in jest. "Let's go, Dalton!"

Deadeye hefted the duffel bag and followed his captain, smirking on the left side of his mouth. "That's *Lieutenant Commander* Dalton to you, Captain Stratosphere."

The crew embarked, stowing their gear in the metal lockers in their sleeping quarters. Sparks went to the engine room to monitor the generators, and Deadeye went to the main saloon to grab a cup of coffee from the galley. He knew he'd be spending some time in the dorsal gun turret on this journey, and he wasn't in a hurry to get up there.

Cipher was already at the comms station when Doc entered the bridge, followed by Jack.

"Hello, gorgeous," Jack muttered, a familiar thrill surging through him as he slid into the pilot's seat. He swung the systems console over to lock into place on his left, outside the throttle controls. Then he noticed the three-axis flight stick he was used to had been replaced with a two-handled control yoke. The throttle also had separate levers for port and starboard lateral thrusters and for each of the large directional turbofans. "This is new," he observed, running his hand over the new controls.

"I hope those won't be a problem," Doc winked, knowing full well that Jack was capable of flying with just about any type of controls conceivable.

"Not at all," he replied, pulling the corded headset from his instrument panel and draping it over his ears. He bent the small microphone arm to point at his chin. "Cipher, what's our status?"

Marissa turned in her seat. "Flight control has cleared us for takeoff, Captain."

"Very good," Jack said. He pressed the *TALK* button on his control console, hailing the engine room. "Bridge to Engine Room. We show power production and batteries nominal. Anything else we should know?"

The voice of the young Kenyan crackled in his ear. "Not at the moment, Captain. The new generators are working at about fifteen percent above previous capacity, as expected."

"Excellent. Maintain station. Crew, prepare for takeoff." Jack cast a look over his left shoulder. "Cipher, notify flight control we are ready for takeoff. Clear ground crew."

The *Daedalus* was uncleated, the ground crew dispersed, and the airship rose gracefully into the crisp air of early morning. As the patchwork of Kenilworth and the adjacent farmland shrank below them, Jack breathed a deep, contented sigh.

Doc slipped out from behind the nav station and stepped down to the left of the pilot's seat. Gently squeezing Jack's shoulder, she leaned in and kissed his cheek. "Have a good flight, handsome."

He looked up at her, a lock of dirty blond hair hanging forward under the headset. His face was lined in soft hues of pink and gold from the sunrise beyond the bridge windows. "This never gets old with you," he winked.

The towns and farms grew ever smaller beneath the ship, and the *Daedalus* soared northward, into a brisk autumn sky.

The prior night's planning had confirmed a course of north-northeast, a total distance of just over 1,853 miles to Nuuk, Greenland's capital city. With the improved dynamos' capacity for power generation, the *Daedalus* could now be expected to maintain a cruising speed of 115 miles per hour, barring headwinds or adverse weather. Reinforcements to the ship's skeleton were already evident in her stability over the St. Lawrence River.

They cleared Quebec and moved over the thick, green forests of Labrador by 1600 hours. When the sun finally dipped below the horizon on their port stern, they were over the Labrador Sea.

With no landmarks or lights below, Jack was forced to rely on compass and instrumentation for the crossing. Fortunately the night was relatively calm, with no severe weather to avoid. Although he was glad of the fact, it set Jack a touch on edge regarding what the rest of the mission might hold for them.

They tied down on a bleak, cold airstrip a mile outside Nuuk just before dawn. Although the ship drew a few curious sightseers after daybreak, the locals ended up wandering away on their own and left the crew alone for the most part.

At 0700 hours, a short, muscular woman appeared on the tarmac with clothing of sealskin and reindeer hide, a leather backpack clutched in one hand. She was perhaps thirty, but looked anywhere from half to twice that, depending on the play of light on her face. She had shoulder-length, coal-black hair, and the tight, well-weathered features of most of the region's indigenous population.

The crew disembarked to re-calibrate and stretch their legs. Cipher accompanied Jack and Doc to welcome the local guide. Her name was Amaruq—meaning "Gray Wolf" in the Inuktitut language. Cipher didn't have much in the way of the Inuit languages and dialects, and it was just as well. Amaruq spoke fluent English with a tinge of Danish accent.

A light fog crept in over the airfield, and Jack had everyone re-embark so they could be underway when the sun broke through. There were roughly the same number of daylight hours as night, given their proximity to the autumnal equinox. From then until late December, the days would be growing steadily shorter.

Doc helped their guide get squared away in her own quarters, which impressed Amaruq to no end. She was used to much more primitive shelter on land. Shedding her cold weather skins in exchange for a plaid flannel shirt and denim trousers, she kept her leather *kamiks* on her feet.

The crew sat in the main saloon and chatted over coffee for a few minutes. Amaruq was a recently-contracted field asset with AEGIS, having been referred by Professor Eric Bjornson, the Copenhagen bureau chief. Her family was several generations established on Greenland's west coast, and she had a cousin in Thule, a small trading village far to the north, who would just be returning with his haul from the summer hunt. He'd have an up-to-date impression of the conditions in the far north.

"Have you ever flown?" Jack asked as he gulped down the last of his coffee.

"Once," Amaruq replied. "On a plane from Qeqertat to our winter hunting lodge in the interior."

Doc raised an eyebrow. "And how did you fare?"

"Kind of like being in a boat," Amaruq said. "After awhile the sickness passes and you just move with it."

"That is how it worked for me," Sparks laughed.

Deadeye grinned. "Same here."

Jack stood and walked his coffee mug to the small kitchenette on the forward port side of the main saloon. He rinsed the enameled tin mug under the spigot and left it to dangle by its handle on a wall hook above the sink. "Welcome aboard the airship *Daedalus*," he said. "You have free run of the craft, except for the engine room, the gun turrets, and the helm chair itself. The exception being when moving through the engine room aft to the cargo bay. When you do, just don't touch any of the control panels or the generators."

Amaruq nodded. "Understood."

Cipher stood and followed Jack's routine at the galley sink. "Does this mean we're departing presently?" she asked.

"It does," said Jack. "All crew to stations. Takeoff in ten."

Sparks disappeared to the engine room, while Deadeye went ashore to uncleat the fore and aft mooring cables. He climbed back aboard as the ship began to drift lazily off the ground.

Cipher took up her seat at comms, while Doc and Amaruq went to the nav station on the starboard side of the bridge. Doc pulled a laminated navigational chart of Greenland from her map cubby and unrolled it on the console.

Amaruq pointed out Thule, off a small inlet in Baffin Bay. Doc took a wax pencil and her T-square, tracing a straight line from Nuuk.

Doing some quick calculations in her head, she scribbled ETAs along the route.

This leg of the trip was just under a thousand miles as the crow flies—990 to be exact—and would take them into the Arctic Circle to the northwest quarter of the island continent.

Jack took the entire eight-hour flight, refusing to let anyone relieve him except for a couple of bathroom breaks. Below them, the deep sapphire bowl of Baffin Bay was interrupted by a thin strip of brown and green, which then gave way to a solid white expanse.

A great icy plain stretched out toward the east, infinite as far as they could see from the bridge windows. Herds of caribou scattered beneath, leaving trails of deep pock marks in the snow. A lone polar bear sunned itself on an ice floe just off the coast, near Sisimiut.

And then the world was blue.

The depths of the Davis Strait lay equally infinite to the west, punctuated by the occasional island or iceberg. Pods of narwhal and beluga undulated through the cold azure water in their various feeding spots, occasional groups of walrus clustered on the floes near the coastline.

The sky was overcast and became darker with a gathering weather system from the west. Jack adjusted course and throttled to full speed for a couple of hours to get ahead of whatever was coming in.

It was just after 1600 hours when they made the final approach on Thule. The sun valiantly attempted to pierce the low clouds, but even with the inconstant light, the small hunting settlement was visible from the air.

Amaruq gasped when she saw the flicker of firelight and long columns of wood smoke bent with the wind. Houses lay in burnt heaps of pallet wood and stone. Reindeer corrals were open, the fences wrecked, gutted carcasses of deer and sled dogs littering the main street. Blood smeared the landscape like a bad mistake in a watercolor painting.

The entire village had been destroyed.

- CHAPTER 6 -

The *Osiris* hovered over the quiet harbor at Murmansk, drifting ever so slightly at its mooring mast. At least two dozen cables tethered the massive airship to weighted docking cleats along its length of more than eight hundred feet.

Thousands of individual amber lights winked from the windows of the sleepy town, which had started life as a busy railroad village during the war. This was northern Russia, on the Kola Bay inlet of the Berents Sea, and the port was strategically located; convenient to northern Europe to the west, and east to Asia.

A subarctic breeze blew in from the bay, and Captain Hummel pulled his uniform jacket tighter at the chest. He stood on the dock, watching the afternoon sunlight on the water as Silver Star field agents scurried to and fro in their various assignments. Smoke encircled his head from the expensive French cigarette between his lips, and he regarded the burly Russian in front of him with a mix of curiosity and disdain.

"I only require to know two things," the Russian grunted in a thickly-accented baritone. "The destination, and the target." His left hand was thrust into the pocket of a worn wool army jacket from the war, a stoppered bottle in his right.

"Major Ivanovitch," Hummel replied, exhaling a stream of perfumed smoke that smelled of cloves and cinnamon, "I can tell you only this: northern Greenland...and the crew of the airship *Daedalus*."

The Russian's eyes bugged from his skull, and he took a long draw from the clear bottle of vodka in his meaty hand. "Captain Stratosphere?" he asked, as if checking to make sure he wasn't imagining things. "Double price."

Hummel had dealt with Russians all his life, and he was used to their way of doing business—especially the shady kind. "You get half when you're aboard. If you are successful, I will guarantee a double bounty on the *Daedalus* crew."

The bearded mercenary nodded, offering the bottle to Captain Hummel. "Is deal. We drink, eh, *tovarisch*?"

"Thank you, no," Hummel dismissed. "You have my word. Go tell your men we cast off in one hour."

Ivanovitch regarded him with a squint, then guzzled another gulp from the bottle, murmuring something about Dutchmen as he wandered off from the docks.

Hummel took the final drag from his smoke and tossed the butt to the ground, extinguishing the ember with the sole of his spit-shined officer's boot.

He despised having to work with Russian freelancers in this way, but reckoned when the piper calls a tune, one must dance with the partner nearest and willing. And he wasn't above making the occasional empty promise to a group of drunken reprobates who lived to fight. No one was forcing them, after all.

As a military man, he valued strategy and tactics above all; however, he was beginning to see a peculiar genius in the way his master Crowley set certain missions into play—missions which, on the surface, were doomed from the start. He might order what appeared to be an ill-advised frontal assault that cost the life of every soldier involved, and yet there was always some valuable bit of intelligence, some new fact gleaned, which would be used to make the next operation that much more effective.

If nothing else, every attack, every strike and feint and parry, helped sow chaos into the ordered world of AEGIS and their governments and laws. Chaos which would one day become the law in and of itself.

As the chill wind closed in on the tiny port of Murmansk, the Black Dog was sure of two things: Aleister Crowley played the long game; and dear God, did Hummel hate Russians.

ଔ

Deadeye hit the frozen ground on both feet, racking the lever on the Winchester as he moved cautiously forward through the carnage.

The airship's outboard turbofans whipped the surface snow and ice into a stinging whirlwind, as he lowered a pair of goggles over his eyes and proceeded to scan the settlement for clues. A swirling layer of smoke blanketed the settlement, coiling into random eddies like serpents on their guard.

Amaruq was next, pulling her fur parka across her front and closing it by threading a series of oblong carved bone shank buttons through their reciprocal leather loops. Her right hand clutched a long, barbed spear with a steel head and a haft hewn from driftwood, carried in a low tracking stance. She followed Deadeye at a brisk pace, abject horror written on her face beneath her own set of snow goggles.

Doc leaped down from the gondola, parka already secure, service revolver in her right hand. The trusty lodestone dangled at the end of a silver chain in her left, twisting in the turbulent wind from the *Daedalus* above.

Jack disembarked last, the fur lining of his gray parka buffeted by the breeze. His goggles were already down, and the arm of a headset microphone protruded from the left side of the hood. The cord fed out from the jacket's collar and around his head to a backpack field radio, one of the newer developments AEGIS always seemed to delight in giving the special operations field teams for practical testing. The whir of the mini-dynamo was all but inaudible above the *Daedalus* engines, and the long whip antenna danced to and fro in the tiny storm they created.

"Okay, Cipher, we're ashore," Jack said into the mic as he pressed the *TALK* switch on the earpiece through the side of the parka's hood. "Take her up to a hundred feet and keep us covered."

"Aye, Captain," crackled Cipher's reply.

If Jack was hesitant to take on the mission without his protégé, Asim "Ace" Al-Hamal, it was mitigated by the fact that Cipher had achieved her Lighter-Than-Air skipper rating from AEGIS Aeronautics back in April, and had become a capable pilot in her own right. She'd also flown the *Daedalus* in a combat situation in the Egyptian desert, and had managed not to crash, nor damage any ship systems.

The ice storm subsided as the ship rose into the air, and Jack followed the others into the center of the settlement, unholstering one of the gleaming Colts from its canvas housing.

Sundered shacks of re-purposed lumber lay strewn about them like a carton of toothpicks dropped on a white kitchen floor. A two-foot section of stove pipe rolled and clattered across the path in front of them, driven by stray wind currents. Bloated mounds of reindeer carrion lay exposed to the elements, collecting thin coats of frost.

Even at this temperature, the smell of death and rot was hard to miss. A few degrees warmer and it would have been overpowering.

Jack moved forward to where Amaruq stood surveying the ghastly scene. "What could have done this?" he asked. "Polar bears?"

The guide squinted behind her goggles and shrugged. "They do not usually raid settlements. Fish and seal are plentiful along the northern coast." Suddenly, something caught her attention, and she pointed to a large mound that Jack had first perceived as a snowdrift. "But there," she said.

As they approached, the mound was revealed to be the dead form of a large adult polar bear, ten feet long, a literal ton of innards coiled on the frozen ground near the bloody, and obviously fatal, belly wound. The impressive predator's white fur was stained red with blood around the mouth and feet. Evidently it had given as good as it got.

"I don't understand," Jack muttered. "Could one bear do all of this?"

Amaruq looked around for more clues. "If it were hungry, or sick, maybe. But..."

"But where are the people?" Doc asked.

Jack scanned the area again and realized she was right. The settlement was devoid of human habitation. "Now that's damn strange."

Doc smiled to herself. In the early stages of their relationship, she and Jack had been on their best behavior. Jack in particular was inherently a squeaky-clean model citizen, never so much as a mild curse on his lips. Doc, on the other hand, had been a battlefield nurse on the Western Front. She knew virtually every dirty word there was, and in several languages to boot.

The last year or two had seen a few more *damn*s and *hell*s from Jack—clearly, she was rubbing off on him.

As she approached the massive carcass, Doc hung the lodestone around her neck and degloved her left hand, holding it a few inches above the massive pile of entrails spilling from the ursine belly. She examined the wound through the tempered glass of her goggles, shaking her head. "No steam, but a tiny amount of residual heat," she observed.

Jack sighed, puzzling as he gazed around. "But where did the people go?"

"If there was more than one bear..." Amaruq began.

"Captain!" came Deadeye's hail from the edge of the settlement.

Jack, Doc, and Amaruq raced to join him as he knelt on the frozen landscape.

"Footprints. At least three different sets that I can make out. Possibly four."

Jack peered into the distance. Multiple sets of human prints indeed trailed off into the white expanse. The streaks of blood went with them. "Think they were giving chase? Tracking another bear?"

Deadeye pushed his goggles to his forehead and inspected the ground before him. A light snow was beginning to waft from the gray clouds overhead, which would make the tracks harder to follow the longer they waited. And there was something else. "I don't see any bear tracks heading out this way."

Doc adjusted her vision to the human footprints leading away into the snow beyond, and realized he was right. Bear prints would be easily spotted in this environment. There just weren't any here.

"I don't understand," Amaruq complained. "If one of them was injured, the interior hunting camps aren't equipped to handle it. And they're mostly gone now, with summer hunting season over."

Doc nodded. "I'd think they'd have taken a boat to one of the coastal settlements."

"Unless they were tracking something," Deadeye said, replacing the goggles on his nose. "Which is this way." Clutching the Winchester in both hands, he stood and marched away into the snow.

The party followed, preparing for an arduous overland trek on foot. Jack knew it might be expedient to have the *Daedalus* pick them up and fly them toward their quarry, but there was too high a probability of missing some small clue along the way.

"Away party to *Daedalus*," Jack said crisply into the microphone. "We're following some human tracks. Fly out a couple miles on our trajectory and see if you find anything."

"Affirmative," Cipher replied, and the great, bullet-shaped shadow passed over them as the airship disappeared into the distance.

The foursome continued at a laborious pace across the icy field of seemingly endless white. It was barely three minutes before Cipher's voice was crackling back into Jack's ear. "We've got something, Captain! About three miles from your position. I count four individuals on foot. Native dress. They look the worse for wear."

"What are they doing?"

"Honestly, sir, they seem to be in some sort of daze. They haven't taken any notice of the ship. Just...trudging in a northeasterly direction."

"Very good, Cipher. Head back and pick us up. You can set us down a bit closer."

A minute later, the *Daedalus* loomed out of the low clouds and dropped down over the flat, white wilderness. The shore party leaped through the side gondola door and kept at the ready, as the airship rose again, banked in a 180-degree turn, and whirred away on its previous heading.

Jack shuffled onto the bridge, loose snow and ice falling from his boots. He'd shrugged clear of the field radio in the main saloon, but left his parka on. The fur-lined hood was down, revealing a navy blue knit watch cap pulled down over his ears, goggles resting atop his brow.

"Some kind of daze, you say?" he asked as he moved alongside the pilot's chair.

Cipher squinted out through the bridge window array, keeping the *Daedalus* nosed down so they could better view the ground on their approach. "Yes sir," she affirmed, throttling back as they cleared a small rise in the ancient volcanic landscape. There, five hundred yards distant, four individuals hobbled through the shin-deep snow on a northeast heading.

"There," Jack said, pointing. "Set us down a couple hundred feet ahead of them." Patting Cipher on the shoulder as he turned to leave, he added, "We'll get to the bottom of this."

"Aye, sir."

Once again, Deadeye dropped from the gondola, carbine gripped in sturdy hands. Doc followed, then Amaruq. Jack brought up the rear, this time leaving the radio pack on board. The airship's twin turbofans created another tornado of blistering ice and snow, and as the away party spread out to meet the approaching strangers, Jack signaled Cipher to climb.

Cipher throttled back the thrust engines and allowed the *Daedalus* to rise gently aloft, swiveling the envelope to pivot around the nose so that she could observe the encounter.

Something about these four bloodied individuals felt off, but she couldn't place what it was, exactly. There was no evidence of another polar bear, so they weren't tracking prey.

At a distance of a hundred feet or so, Jack gestured briefly at Deadeye. "Hold up here, Charlie. Keep a clear field of fire."

The sharpshooter held his carbine at waist level, taking up a position far to their left, where he could cover the group without worrying about hitting one of his own crewmates.

As Jack moved toward the front of the group, Doc caught his arm.

"Jack, look," she said, a tremor in her voice that wasn't a result of the cold. "The lodestone."

As Jack glanced at the crystalline shard hanging around Doc's neck, he noticed the familiar blue-white light and the high-pitched hum. The narrow end was pointed outward in a straight angle toward the approaching group of natives, and almost seemed to tug away from her body.

"Got the brace on?" he asked, referring to the ancient bronze armor piece gifted to her in Greece by AEGIS patron Marina Stavros.

Doc nodded. "Spoke the incantation this morning."

"Good," Jack grumbled. "There's clearly some strong magic at work here. Let's keep our eyes open."

Doc nodded again, right hand going to her hip with the canvas holster.

Amaruq pressed forward, worried and bewildered. These were her kinsmen, her cousin and his party who had been breaking down the summer hunting camps and preserving harvested meat for the winter. What had happened back in Thule?

"Anarsi?" she called.

The natives halted in their tracks. They stood silently, swaying in the frosty air, sealskin clothing shredded and drenched in blood. Savage wounds were evident across the party, exposed skin pale and puckered with cold.

As Amaruq took in the group, she noted for the first time that the center-most man had a gaping horizontal wound in his abdomen, from which a colorful curtain of intestines and viscera dangled, frozen and brittle.

Amaruq stood stiff in place, every natural danger sense in her body triggered like a shift whistle in a factory. This was bad.

Jack and Doc approached behind her, spread out and hands gripping holsters, ready for what they feared was an inevitable showdown with some sort of dark magic. Still, they knew they needed more information before leaping into action.

Amaruq took a cautious step forward in the snow. The man with the apron of guts suddenly looked up at her, eyes glowing a fiery emerald green that illuminated the darkness of his hooded parka.

"Anarsi," Amaruq repeated, "what has happened?"

Another set of green-lit eyes blinked in her direction, then another. The fourth native slowly raised his hooded head, revealing a skull grinning through brutalized flesh, the same pinpoints of blazing green light searing from within the eye sockets.

And then they charged.

- CHAPTER 7 -

The four hunters became a writhing, snarling mass of clawing hands and gnashing teeth, scrambling forward in their blood-stained furs. Amaruq's eyes grew wide and her breath caught in her throat. It was impossible to scream even if she'd wanted to.

For men clearly dead, they were impossibly quick—four pairs of hands were on her within moments, tearing at her coat and grabbing her face and hair.

A shot from Deadeye's Winchester peeled the rearmost hunter from the pack, sending him spinning a few steps backward. Ratcheting the lever, Charlie sent the empty brass casing into the snow, and raised the rifle to fire a second time.

Jack leaped forward, Colt already cocked and in his hand. Amaruq was hunched over, her back to the marauding undead. Thrusting the barrel of the .45 under the hood of the nearest hunter, he approximated where the forehead would most likely be, and squeezed the trigger. An eruption of skull fragments and brain matter exploded out the back of the hood, and Jack withdrew the pistol, bracing for the hunter's body to crumple to the crunchy white ground.

When the hooded head settled forward instead, green embers glaring at him, Jack knew they were in trouble. "Stay back!" he warned, whether to his crew or the attackers he wasn't sure.

Ignoring the warning, Doc moved forward into the fray, throwing her arm over Amaruq. As the punishing hands continued their assault, the air around the two women flashed a luminescent aquamarine, visually warping in a spherical shape. The ancient armor piece fulfilled its function, absorbing the kinetic impact of the incoming attacks.

"Get back to the ship!" Jack ordered, emptying the Colt's magazine into the attackers as he unsnapped the second holster on his left.

With her arm across Amaruq and the magic vambrace invoked, Doc guided her charge toward the *Daedalus*, hovering a hundred feet back and fifty feet in the air.

The hunters turned their focus to Jack, who drew the second Colt and began firing. Cold, viscous blood spattered, bits of dead flesh flew, and still they pressed on him, clutching at his parka, slamming him with bony fists. Two whose jaws were still attached tried to bite at his arms. Jack gauged them surprisingly strong—and he knew something about fighting the undead.

The hunter Deadeye had drawn away from the group with his first shot turned and charged him, coursing across the snowy plain, green eyes aglow. The Winchester barked in a continuous volley, Charlie racking the lever, firing, racking, firing. Every impact blew holes in the approaching figure, sending bits of tissue and clothing into the crisp evening air.

He tightened his aim to concentrate on the hunter's head, pumping round after round into the attacker's skull, until his parka's hood lay tattered in strips of sealskin and fox fur and the lower half of his head was sheared away.

Still the hunter lumbered toward him.

Jack emptied the second pistol's magazine, already scrambling backward toward the ship. He could see Doc and Amaruq in the lead, some forty feet distant. The hunters still pressed toward him, but his last volley had created some much-needed space. A few more paces, just a few more...

Suddenly the sleek bullet nose of the *Daedalus* swooped down over him, and Jack dove into the snow, throwing his arms over his head. In the cockpit, Cipher lined up the forward-facing Lewis guns with the fire-linked secondary joystick and gripped the trigger. Four machine guns spat a stream of hot lead and red tracers into the three hunters pushing toward Jack, ripping mercilessly through them. Body parts perforated and exploded away, leaving an assortment of extremities and a light crimson carpet on the pale ground.

Deadeye racked the Winchester and squeezed the trigger, and the hollow click told him he was empty. The last attacker was too far away from the others to have been brought down in the Lewis gun barrage, and too close to Charlie to make an effective target for the *Daedalus*. He was now in close combat with a dead man who didn't know he was dead.

Recalling the trench-sweeping missions he was often assigned on the Western Front, Deadeye instantly reversed his arm position, swinging the butt of the Winchester up to hit the attacker square in the chest. It didn't stop him, nor did Charlie expect it to, but it slowed the man's progress just enough to allow a shift of stance. Pivoting back on his right leg,

Deadeye planted his left foot in the snow, then slid his right back in a slight crouch. His right hand choked up on the carbine's walnut grip, and he drew it back behind his shoulder with the heavy stock above his head.

The undead marauder recovered its momentum and surged forward, hands clawing. Charlie swung the rifle like a Louisville Slugger baseball bat, and the hunter's head sailed away into the air with a pronounced pop.

Deadeye blinked in disbelief as the headless corpse continued to stagger and clutch at the air around it. At least he was able to gain some distance, and as he retreated toward his comrades, Cipher hovered the *Daedalus* over to the decapitated hunter and lit it up with a blaze of blistering lead and red tracers.

As Charlie backed away from the carnage, he could see that even the disembodied limbs continued to twitch and move in the snow, and he knew they were up against some of the darkest magic they'd ever encountered.

The *Daedalus* came around and descended between the landing party and the pulverized remains of the undead hunters. Amaruq wiped her eyes on the sleeve of her parka as the wind from the airship's thrusters whipped around them.

Each member of the crew was thinking, *What the hell did we just encounter?* but they all boarded in silence, collecting in the main saloon and leaving the question unsaid. Jack shrugged out of his parka, Doc and Deadeye following his lead. He went to the galley wall and thumbed a switch on the intercom. "We're aboard, Cipher. Take us up to two thousand feet and maintain a northeastern course at half speed."

Cipher's voice crackled out of the speaker. "Affirmative."

Jack grabbed one of the lacquered metal mugs from the hooks over the galley counter, filling it with coffee from the percolator pot as the ship rose again, fighting a stiff evening breeze from the coast. Finally he regarded the assembled group in their various positions around the starboard settee, noticing their guide pensive and clouded over in grief.

"Anarsi…" Amaruq sobbed quietly. "Anarsi, why?"

Deadeye frowned. Doc and Jack exchanged an uncertain look, as Amaruq blinked at them through a veil of tears.

"Amaruq," Doc sighed. "What do you know that you aren't telling us?"

The Inuit guide clamped her eyes shut, trying to wish away the world. "I've only heard stories, never encountered them before…"

"Encountered *what* before?" Jack growled.

Amaruq fixed him in a cold stare that made the hair on the nape of his neck stand on end. "What do you know of the *draug*?"

Deadeye scratched his temple and squinted. "The what now?"

Jack's look was blank, but then he left the history and occult lore to his lovely partner. Doc's eyes slowly grew wide, and he knew she had something.

"*Draug*," she repeated. "Is that related to the *draugr*? The Viking legend?"

Amaruq shut her eyes and nodded. "*Draugr* is the Old Norse plural. Danes and Inuit know them as the *draug*."

Jack looked at Doc expectantly, but she kept her eyes focused on the young Greenlander.

"Viking warriors resurrected by occult means to continue their battle in Midgard," Amaruq explained.

Doc sighed. "They could find no rest, no solace in food or earthly pleasure," she said. "They're essentially ghouls. Reanimated corpses whose only drive is to kill."

"Lovely," Deadeye snorted, ambling to the galley for his own cup of coffee. He exchanged a look with Amaruq, who nodded in the affirmative, and he pulled down two mugs, filling them from the coffee pot.

"I grew up hearing the legends," Amaruq continued. "The Inuit have a very strong storytelling tradition. We have the *qivitoq* and similar legends, like most cultures have some tradition of resurrected dead. Some of the local clans speak of a *siku toqu*, or ice corpse."

Deadeye returned to the settee and put one of the mugs on the table in front of Amaruq. She smiled at him and added a quiet, "Thanks."

Doc tilted her head at an inquisitive angle. "Interesting that you would choose to invoke the *draug* over the Inuit legends, seeing as how those hunters were your own kin…"

Amaruq pursed her lips tightly, brow furrowed in concentration. "I am Inuit, yes, but I am *Kalaallit Nunaat*—a Greenlander. And Greenlanders share Inuit and Danish cultural traditions." Her gaze fell to the perforated aluminum floor panels of the saloon, and she added quietly, "But there was something…not of Inuit origin about those hunters."

"What do you mean?" asked Doc.

Amaruq searched for the right words, beginning to speak at least twice before she finally assembled her point. "Whatever brought Anarsi back from the dead, it felt…foreign…somehow. Not of our culture, not like the *qivitoq*. They felt completely alien to me."

Doc suddenly tensed and stood from the settee, causing Jack to stumble backward, fighting to keep from spilling his coffee.

"That's it!" she exclaimed, face bright with instant mania.

Jack squinted at her, protecting his coffee mug. "That's what?"

"Amaruq," Doc began. "You said it felt alien to you. And we already knew there was a high probability that the radio signal was non-terrestrial in origin."

"Yet to be verified," Jack cautioned, "but go on."

"What if this signal isn't a greeting?" Doc proposed. "What if the signal is arcane in nature? What if..." she trailed off, losing some of her manic excitement in a dark realization. "What if the signal is reanimating the dead?"

Deadeye blinked, amazed and on high alert. He backed away from the saloon and exited to the bridge, mumbling something about getting Cipher in on this particular discussion.

Jack looked absolutely dumbfounded, but it appeared Doc's hypothesis was meeting with Amaruq's approval.

"That follows," Amaruq nodded. "The signal might just be a conveyance for the magic to reach its intended targets."

"Wait a second," Jack interrupted. "Hold on, sister. Its intended targets? Like who?"

"How about four Inuit hunters recently mauled to death by a polar bear?" Doc frowned. "Just for starters."

Jack wasn't convinced. "But how is it reaching them, and only them?"

"Jack, you know as well as I that you don't need a radio receiver to pick up a signal." Doc thrust her hands on her hips in a lecturing stance. "We're bombarded with radio waves all the time."

"I know that," Jack acknowledged. "But if this is a magic spell, why isn't it affecting us?"

"Because we're not dead," Amaruq answered dryly.

Jack scrunched his face like a child being made to eat Brussels sprouts for the first time. "I mean, why isn't it affecting more people?"

Doc took a deep breath and sighed. "How do we know it's not?"

Jack sensed the profound wisdom in that rhetorical question before she'd finished asking it, and a sense of inevitable doom washed over him like a cold shower. Here was some kind of transmitter—possibly of alien origin—sending out, not a welcome or a handshake, but a rebuttal to the angel of death. And all they had to do was locate this beacon of unholy resurrection and secure it before agents of the Silver Star used the device to its logical extension by raising an entire army of corpses to create a literal hell on Earth.

He'd had butterflies on missions before. He was used to them. That slight unease kept him alert and on his toes. Kept him alive. But this was starting to feel a bit hopeless, and that was a feeling he did not like. Not one little bit.

Cipher entered the main saloon and went immediately to the galley to pour her own coffee. "What did I miss of the conversation?"

"Oh not much," Jack mused. "We're apparently going after the source of a signal that brings the dead back to life."

Cipher gave the group a quizzical look, dropping a small cube of sugar into the coffee.

Doc winked at her. "You know, the usual."

- CHAPTER 8 -

The *Daedalus* probed northeast on its course, port and starboard running lights flashing red and green in the bleak gray night. Despite the absence of sun in the sky, the airship's forward halogen lamps reflected off the thickening atmosphere as a new weather system moved down from the north.

Jack steadied the flight controls and fought the crosswind, the bridge rattling with each new gust. It was as if the region itself was telling them to go home. There would be nothing for them but bitter cold and death, or worse, if they insisted on pushing ahead.

Amaruq sat at Doc's nav station, ostensibly to assist Jack in plotting the course, but at this point he knew what direction they were headed, and was just trying to find a break in the weather, so she sat back and observed. Deadeye sat at the radio console, headset over his right ear as he kept the band tuned on the regular signal from their destination. It was right on time, beginning at 6 p.m. sharp and repeating for ten minutes before shutting off abruptly.

"No change?" asked Jack.

"Negative, Cap'n," Deadeye replied. "The source of the signal has not moved."

Jack glanced over at the altimeter, noting that they were maintaining about a thousand feet, but that they were expending ever more power to do so. As the exterior temperature plummeted, the air became denser and the lift gases aboard the *Daedalus* contracted, resulting in lower buoyancy, even with Sparks' newly-implemented heating system.

The four lateral thrust engines outside the airship's envelope were already spinning at full throttle. He angled the giant outboard thrusters downward about thirty degrees to assist the lift gas in keeping the ship aloft, simultaneously thumbing the *TALK* button on his own radio console.

"Attention, crew," he huffed into his headset as another blast of frozen wind shook and buffeted the sleek outer hull. "Gonna want to stay strapped in if you can. Weather's getting worse, and we're only maintaining any kind of altitude with thruster assist." He nervously fished a stick of licorice chewing gum from his shirt pocket, unwrapped it, and crammed it into his mouth. "We may have a fight on our hands."

Deadeye knew he meant the weather, but couldn't help but think the comment could also refer to the impending sense of mortal danger everyone was feeling. He could almost feel the ice collecting on the hull as the ship's engines whined under the stress of the blistering northern winds.

In the map room, Doc and Cipher poured over copious AEGIS research on the Martian language. Doc had already spent most of the year familiarizing herself with the strange script, its mix of fluid and angular symbols, similar to Babylonian or Akkadian cuneiform.

With some prompting and guidance from Cipher, she'd begun to discern a sort of rudimentary alphabet. There was only one problem: there was no way to associate the radio signal with the written symbols without a translation, some form of auditory Rosetta Stone.

Still, Doc insisted to herself, it might be quite beneficial to know the written instructions for *STOP*, to power down whatever piece of alien technology they might stumble upon. "If only there was some kind of key," she muttered.

Cipher raised an eyebrow. "But where would we start? We could assign a tonal frequency to a glyph and run it high to low, or vice versa, but we'd run the risk of literally getting it backwards."

Doc leaned back in her chair and rubbed her eyes. "At least I'll have some idea of how to operate whatever is making that broadcast. Just wish I knew more."

Pencils jumped and clattered on the desk as the ship took a wallop from the crosswind.

Cipher stood, bracing herself on the chart table for stability. "I guess that's my signal to get back to the radio."

Doc blinked, staring at Cipher with an instant look of incredulity. "Hold on," she said, a smile creeping across her bow lips. "Cipher, you're giving me all sorts of great ideas."

"Ma'am?" Cipher frowned, cocking her head in confusion.

Doc sorted through the papers on the table to produce one of the printed representations of the signal waveform from the AEGIS listening station oscilloscopes. She pointed at the jagged shape on the page, tracing the zigzag pattern with a slender finger. "See there? At the end of the signal? How there's a tone of the lowest frequency used?"

Cipher leaned over, following Doc's finger across the paper with interest. "Right."

"You're not an occultist," Doc continued, staring at the page, "but you know language. In my years of studying various arcana from around the world, I've found several commonalities. At the end of most spells, there is some kind of special keyword, an invocation that sets the magic in motion. Not unlike an archer loosing the bowstring."

Cipher's hazel-brown eyes brightened in the dim light of the map room. "I think I take your meaning."

"All we have to do is reach the source, observe it during a broadcast, note its configuration on that 'invocation', then reverse it."

"Oh, is that all?" Cipher answered in her particular brand of wry sarcasm.

"It's hopeless, isn't it?"

"Well I wouldn't go that far—"

"Don't patronize me, Cipher. It's hopeless." Doc's mind had run ahead on her track of logic and found it impossibly long and convoluted.

So many steps, so many variables.

She had just started to rub her eyes again when the ship was knocked almost sideways by a massive gust of wind, sending Cipher against the wall, hugging her shoulders with a grunt.

Lights flickered twice before shutting off. The room was suddenly awash in red emergency lighting. A strained hum from the outboard thrusters could be heard through their airfoil arms, reverberating throughout the aluminum structure.

"Get back to the bridge," Doc ordered, standing from the map table and rushing to the open doorway. "I'll check the engine room!"

Cipher pushed herself from the corner of the map room and disappeared forward, while Doc hustled aft to the engineering station.

The main gondola corridor was bathed in crimson hazard light, the air abuzz with shouts over the ship's intercom.

"We're losing power," Jack's voice erupted over the speakers. "Sparks, I need a status report!"

"Fighting the storm is putting a strain on the battery array," was the reply, tinged with Dhakiya Kitur's native Kenyan inflection. "Decrease throttle or we'll have to cut the heat to the ballonets!"

As Doc twisted the hatch door handle and stepped into the engine room, a festival of flickering lights and arcing electrical embers met her eyes, and she froze.

"Affirmative," Jack answered over the intercom speaker. "Cutting throttle."

Almost as soon as he'd said it, a rooster tail of bright sparks exploded from one of the new voltage monitors, and an entire bank of buttons and gauges went dark. The whine of the thrusters deepened and slowed.

Doc stepped into the small room dominated by a central island at dining table height, which held ten Edison-DiMarco frictionless dynamos in two banks of five. The walls were outlined in work counters, control consoles, and endless panels of gauges.

"How can I help?" she asked frantically.

Sparks cast a dubious look at her. "Get on the intercom with the bridge. I need to restart the entire system!"

Doc's stomach fell as the *Daedalus* was pushed and pounded by the crosswind, no longer able to fight back. She knew what a hard restart meant. All electrical systems—save that of emergency battery power—would be shut down and turned back on, one at a time. That meant propulsion, heating, radio, internal comms...literally everything but the inboard lighting.

Leaning onto the control desk nearest the hatchway, she held down the *TALK* button on the intercom, speaking into the microphone hidden beneath the metal lattice of the rectangular speaker cover.

"Doc here, in engineering," she greeted urgently. "Sparks needs to do a hard restart of the main power."

"Is there any way to keep control systems on-line?" came Jack's reply, a note of terror in his voice.

Doc threw a glance toward the other end of the room, and Sparks shook her head no. Another panel erupted in a shower of dead circuits, and dimmed out.

"Negative!" Doc answered, leaning with the ship as it was battered repeatedly by the frozen winds. "Circuits are failing! Taking all power off-line now!"

Sparks switched the main breaker off and everything went dark, except for the sinister red glow of the emergency lamps.

With the engines dead, the ship tossed and rattled on the winds, completely at their mercy. The ice-encrusted envelope formed an indentation in its spine, becoming curved like a hot dog as the internal ballonets contracted in the cold.

The *Daedalus* had been on a northeast heading, but now it was slammed almost due east, forced to ride wherever and for however long the stormy current decided to take her.

On the bridge, Jack fought the controls out of habit, but it made no difference. Cipher clipped the lap belt into place at the radio console, while Deadeye gripped the edge of the navigation desk.

Amaruq was already strapped into the chair. All four watched as a world of stark white and gray zipped by horizontally outside the bridge window array.

Suddenly, the ship lunged forward, and Jack felt the tailwind surge up behind them. One by one, lights began to flicker to life on the pilot's console. He had lateral thrust. As the wind continued pushing them off course, Jack slowly throttled forward. Their altitude was now five hundred feet and dropping. The fore and aft thrusters weren't doing a lot of good, but at least Jack felt like he was being useful in mitigating some of the storm's brutality.

Four hundred feet, and dropping.

In the distance, a wall of dark gray was split with a vertical blank space of somewhat-lighter-gray, upon which was projected a brilliant luminescent dance of green-blue light. Jack knew it to be the *Aurora Borealis*—the Northern Lights—the visual result of solar winds rippling across the Earth's magnetic field. The effect in this case was muted by the ice and snow whirling about them. Every snowflake was a grain of static obscuring this shimmering, multicolored glow.

Judging by the geometric puzzle placed before him, it looked as if they were staring into a canyon, with steep walls on either side and no good way around.

The canyon rim seemed much higher than their current altitude of two hundred fifty feet, and there was nothing they could do about gaining altitude with the ballonet heating system out of commission. He could try to negotiate a course through the canyon, risking hull damage and possibly death on the craggy, ice-encrusted granite. Or he could adjust course to the east and see if there was another way to get north, past this range of mountains.

Something deep within his conscience told him that forging ahead through the canyon with a disabled ship in foul Arctic weather would not be the most prudent course. Nor would the easterly option, which would sap precious time from their aggressive schedule. He'd flown in severe weather enough to know that, despite being the skilled pilot he was, he ultimately couldn't outguess Mother Nature—or outfly her.

Their tailwind picked up, sending the *Daedalus* pitching forward as Jack desperately worked the flight yoke. There was a dull *crack* as a control aileron snapped, starboard tail flap fluttering loose on its hinge.

The cold, flat gray of the canyon loomed out of the blustery night, barely two hundred yards distant.

Another light blinked on his console: he now had the main thrusters.

Altitude check: one hundred feet.

Jack nudged the powerful thrust engines to half-speed. The airship listed to port, fighting the oppressive, bitter winds. The canyon rim had grown taller than their field of view, let alone their maximum altitude.

Comms were still out. He'd made it plain that flight controls were the priority, and Sparks was seeing to that. "Heads up, folks!" Jack warned, glancing at his flight gauges.

Altitude: fifty feet.

Gray walls of snow-streaked granite blocked either side of the window array. A dull white carpet flashed up at them.

Twenty-five feet.

The tailwind caught them once more, and the canyon entrance was dead ahead. Jack tried to guide the ship down delicately with both lateral engines and the giant thrusters. But then the crosswind returned, whipping the *Daedalus* around and slamming it into the side of the canyon mouth.

The main cabin roared and shook with the impact, sending the occupants against the nearest surface or straining against safety harnesses. Anything not secured in the gondola clattered to the floor.

Ten feet.

The airship groaned an almost-human sound of agony, nosing down toward the frozen earth. There was a sound like the opening of a giant soup tin, and everything was suddenly very cold, and very white.

- CHAPTER 9 -

Bitter, icy winds whistled through the canyon mouth, the evening storm showing no sign of abating soon. The *Daedalus* leaned against the granite wall, starboard thruster pod half-buried in snow.

The envelope was bent, not only with the top indentation from the shrinking gas ballonets, but from its sideways impact with the canyon on its descent. Interior emergency lights bled through the gondola windows, bathing the surrounding landscape in an eerie crimson glow. A pair of forward exterior headlights illuminated the first twenty yards of the canyon entrance before it disappeared into the distance.

One by one, exterior hatches popped open, and parka-clad figures exited the ship, scanning their surroundings with the beams of flashlights.

Deadeye hefted the dorsal hatch and set it open, noting the damage as he peered around. He climbed onto the vulcanized canvas skin—now gritty with a layer of icy snow—and clipped a security line onto the rail running aft from the hatch to the tail assembly.

Jack exited through the port gondola side door, having to leap several feet to the ground due to the ship being heeled over against the cliff side. Sparks followed, and they separated to take stock of the condition of the vessel.

The brutal wind blowing through the canyon had built up a sizable snowdrift at its mouth, and Jack found himself wading up to his thighs as he moved toward the ship's nose.

Sparks trudged aft, the beam from her rectangular electric torch roaming the contours of the craft. The port stern seemed in good shape; it was the starboard side, with its possible impact damage, that she worried most about.

After their cursory visual inspection, Jack and Sparks hauled out the pneumatic piton drivers used to anchor the ship in barren or rocky terrain. Even if it could fly, Jack reasoned, he didn't want it tossed around against the canyon cliffs like a scrap of newspaper in the wind.

With cables fore and aft, and the ship secure, the crew reassembled in the main saloon, breathing warmth into cupped hands and sipping hot coffee. Amaruq, Doc, and Cipher stood in various corners of the room, observing the other three as they compared damage reports. There was power enough to run the heating and galley electrical systems, but even so, there seemed to be a draft.

"Nose looks okay," Jack began. "No apparent hull damage, turret is good, external lighting intact. Got a few scrapes on the starboard envelope. Easy patches."

Sparks nodded in agreement. "Stern is a bit more of a problem," she added. "Got a snapped control cable and the starboard horizontal stabilizer's loose."

Deadeye pursed his lips, eyes squinting in a pensive look. "Envelope is slightly caved in, topside," he drawled. "Dorsal turret has got a cracked cowling and a bad hydraulic line, and it looks like the starboard side skeleton is bent from impact."

"We can probably lose the dorsal turret, spike the guns, and free up some weight," Jack offered.

"I don't like losing our main defensive option in the sky," Deadeye worried, "but those two guns alone are over a hundred pounds, and the whole structure is another hundred at least."

Nodding, Jack assured Charlie, "I'll make sure if anyone finds them, they can only be used as scrap metal."

"Sounds like a couple days' repair, at least," Doc asserted.

Jack filled his mug from the coffee pot for the second time in five minutes. "I'd say so. Sparks?"

Sparks clamped a cold left hand in her right armpit as she sipped her coffee. She nodded back at him. "Sounds about right, if I have some help."

"You'll have it," Jack promised. "Now, Amaruq, what can you tell us about this canyon?"

The young woman sighed, eyes downcast. "We call it *Gooroq Aniaat*, the Valley of Pain."

"Of course it is," Jack muttered.

Deadeye folded his arms across his chest. "Why can't we ever explore the Valley of Tranquil Summer Afternoons?"

"I'm sure the Cherokee have no colorful place names?" Amaruq shot back.

Deadeye lowered his head immediately. "Fair enough," he admitted quietly.

Amaruq continued. "The mountain range forms the natural barrier between our ancestral hunting lands and the region of the *Nanoq Inuk*. The White Bear People."

Doc pursed her lips in thought. "So your people don't go beyond the canyon mouth?"

Amaruq shook her head of raven hair in the negative. "As a general rule, it is forbidden." She took a sip of warm coffee, feeling the collective disappointment in the room. "But I've been beyond it," she added quietly.

Jack perked up, eyes wide. "Well now, here's something!"

"About ten years ago," she explained, "I was with my cousin, Anarsi, and his father, Pilo. We were tracking caribou and got caught in a sudden storm. The caribou herded into the canyon, so we followed them. By the time the storm lifted, we'd made it to the other end, and found the caribou had been taken by strange men in bear furs and old Viking armor."

Doc and Jack exchanged a look.

Amaruq finished her story, eyes still on the metal grate of the main saloon floor. "Uncle Pilo challenged the Bear People, and they cut him down. Anarsi and I were young, and so was their leader. He let us go, with enough of the meat to survive the journey back." She reached down the front of her shirt and fished out a small pendant on a leather thong: a

Thor's hammer carved from walrus ivory, the hammer dangling from its handle.

Doc whistled in appreciation of the simple artifact. "What is that?"

"He said it would protect us on our journey back, and if we ever found ourselves lost again..."

Doc's eyes were bright and Jack could tell she was excited about the prospect of another culture, even more remote than the Inuit, living at the top of the globe. "Do you know what this means?"

"I think so," Jack grunted. "We have to get to the other side of the canyon and make contact."

Sparks tossed back the final sip of her coffee. "As long as I have some more hands, I don't mind not being out in that, on foot."

Jack nodded in agreement. "Oh, I don't blame you, Sparks. But we can use the Dugdale, and haul a sled behind." He referred to the lightweight electric motorcycle carried in the *Daedalus* cargo bay, which had been modified for snow travel with skis on the front fork and a twin track system in place of the rear wheel.

The canvas-and-aluminum fold-out sidecar was braced at the bottom with another ski for stability. They already carried a sled made from a hollow aluminum frame and a lightweight canvas floor, much like the deck of a catamaran.

"I hate to bring this up, Captain Stratosphere," Doc interjected, "but I think you're going to be staying behind to help Sparks make repairs."

Jack felt like he'd been punched in the sternum. "I-I'm sorry, what was that?" he stammered.

Doc moved toward him, gently caressing his shoulder with a delicate hand. "As the only one remotely qualified to handle an occult artifact of this nature, I have to go."

He knew the words before she spoke them, and each one made his ears burn and cheeks flush red.

"I need Cipher in case we need to communicate with people speaking a Norse dialect. Deadeye is the best tracker, and Amaruq knows the local area. That leaves you here."

It hurt at first. He was always the first to volunteer for hazard duty, no matter what the locale or potential dangers involved. This felt somehow like a blow to his command at best, his manhood at least. But as he mulled everything over in his head, he came to a serene place within.

From a purely practical standpoint, Doc was absolutely right. Aside from Sparks, and Rivets before her, Jack had the most technical expertise when it came to the *Daedalus*-class light reconnaissance airship, and this one was in dire shape. It was clearly he who should stay behind with the engineer.

"You're right," he agreed. "I don't like splitting up, but we need to get the ship back in the air, and we can't lose precious time on the ground waiting for repairs." He recalled the crew meeting before he and Doc had gone into the lost valley in the Himalayas just two years previous. It had almost gotten ugly. He didn't want that to happen here. "You four get a good start, and Sparks and I will get *Daedalus* sky-worthy again."

His reserved tone and acquiescence was unexpected, and Doc took him aside as the others traded looks of confusion and concern.

"You sure you're okay, honey?"

Jack shrugged. "It's the rational thing," he sighed. "Just be careful out there. Don't take any..."

"Unnecessary risks?" she finished for him. "Aside from this basic endeavor, I promise not to look for more trouble."

Jack wrapped her in his broad arms and hugged her tightly, and as they separated, Doc planted a passionate kiss on his open mouth.

The crew immediately began to pace the saloon and chat among themselves. They knew Jack and Doc as a couple, but over the last couple of missions, they'd been keeping less of a barrier between work and their romantic relationship—not that anyone minded, particularly. But they were clearly sharing a moment here. A moment best shared in private.

"Get your gear," Jack said, holding Doc's arms gently. "And don't die."

Doc winked mischievously. "Oh? What if I do?"

"You don't have permission," Jack said in mock seriousness. "I'd have to report you to AEGIS Admin for insubordination. They'd probably drum you out of the organization."

Doc chuckled. "I'll take that under advisement."

As the storm began to blow over with the arrival of a bleak new morning, the crew donned their thick parkas and cold weather gear. Sparks rigged the sled for supplies and passengers with a short tow cable from the rear of the Dugdale.

Deadeye sat astride the motorcycle, with Amaruq in the sidecar. Cipher sat toward the rear of the sled, with Doc gripping the very back like a musher in the All Alaska Sweepstakes.

Jack and Sparks watched as their four comrades disappeared into the hazy distance under a pale dawn light. They turned to each other and nodded in silent agreement, then retreated into the relative safety of the cargo bay. Sparks continued on into the engine room, while Jack hit the button for the giant, whining hydraulic arms to lift the cargo bay door closed with a resounding *thud*.

- CHAPTER 10 -

After the incessant whirling of the razor-sharp, icy storm winds which had forced the *Daedalus* to crash at the canyon mouth, passage through its center was eerily quiet.

A cone of white light scanned the dim valley in front of the Dugdale as its electric dynamo whined through the fresh dusting of snow. Without a tow-load, the lightweight motorcycle had a top speed of fifty miles per hour. With the added weight of the snow treads, the supply sled, and two additional passengers, it was significantly less. The bike struggled along at a haggard pace, front fork skidding back and forth on the ice pack beneath the snow, as the four explorers braced against the numbing cold.

The canyon was unnaturally straight, roughly a hundred feet wide and at least five miles long before it opened at the other side into the bleak white unknown. The sky began to brighten as the sun peered above the horizon. Almost instantly, the canyon valley was socked in with a cold fog, and Charlie was forced to slow the converted motorcycle even more.

About halfway through, Deadeye noted the canyon suddenly converged toward a choke point. Because of the fog, he couldn't see it until they were almost in its center. The passage narrowed to a round opening perhaps thirty feet wide, a massive snow bridge arcing across the top of the canyon like a frozen suture in a giant wound.

All eyes scanned the limits of what the fog would allow. Deadeye slowed the Dugdale to a crawl as they threaded the needle. They emerged through the choke point, and Charlie felt himself ripped from the seat of the motorcycle and thrown like a rag doll into the snowbank on his right.

He rolled across the ice-dusted trail, coming up into a crouch, trying to gather his bearings and take stock of the situation. The motorcycle tottered along, curving left toward the canyon wall.

Cipher was already off the sled and sprinting to jump into the bike's saddle. Then a shadow fell across his face, and he gazed upward into the glowing green eyes of a frozen corpse, the rusted nose guard of a 10th century Viking helm resting above sinister, grinning teeth.

The skeletal assailant was clad in rusty chainmail and shredded leather armor. It held no weapon, merely extending its bony, talon fingers. An eerie, high-pitched wheeze erupted from its frozen throat, sounding like a cross between a hissing cat and breaching dolphin. Deadeye could not be sure of its source, for there were surely no lungs within this animated cadaver.

Charlie instantly took inventory. His Winchester was slung on the motorcycle, now heading toward the left side of the canyon at a slow crawl. That left what he had on his person: a hunting knife on his left hip—not too effective. Acting purely on muscle-memory, he reached to his right and drew the JoLoAr .45 from its canvas holster and squeezed off an immediate shot. He'd acquired the strange-looking firearm in Madrid a couple of years ago, its selling points being the lack of a trigger guard, and an unconventional cocking spur on the side that made it possible for mounted troops to use single-handed.

His bullet entered the face of the undead Viking just under the cheekbone, shattering out the base of the skull to no discernible effect.

The creature hissed again and lunged forward, and Deadeye rolled away. As he came up this time, he could see Cipher had regained control of the Dugdale, and was using the motorcycle to pin another *draug* to the icy canyon wall as Amaruq stood in the sidecar, brandishing a bone-tipped harpoon like she was hunting seal. Doc ran out of the fog to Charlie's left, the ethereal blue glow of the lodestone lighting her way. Her revolver was already in her hands as she stepped up behind the skeletal warrior and fired just under the metal helm at point blank range. The bullet glanced off the ancient armor and away into the canyon behind her, and the creature whipped a mighty claw around to its left, sending Doc tumbling to the snow with a grunt.

Deadeye moved toward her, but the *draug* stepped to its left, blocking the way. Another pair of emerald ember eyes appeared out of the fog behind him, and Charlie felt the weight of the grave as a third reanimated Viking corpse leaped onto his back.

A creature of instinct, Deadeye suddenly felt years of high school wrestling and Army close combat training flood his consciousness. Before he knew it, he was falling to a forward crouch, hauling down on the attacker's bony arms, sending the *draug* over his head and crashing into the first.

He sprinted the handful of yards to Doc's side, hauling her upright. "Come on, Doc!" he shouted, the words echoing through the canyon as they rallied to the motorcycle.

The Dugdale's small, reactionless dynamo whined pitifully as Cipher cracked the throttle wide open, having pinned the third *draug* against the cold granite wall of the canyon. Amaruq had successfully removed its skull with the broad head of the bone harpoon, but the thing's arms continued to slash and strike at the women with abandon.

"Go!" Deadeye called to Cipher, waving her away down the canyon valley. "Get moving!"

Cipher closed the bike throttle, and together she and Amaruq hauled the motorcycle back from the frozen wall. The headless corpse lunged forward immediately, but Amaruq hooked the harpoon barb under one skeletal leg and hauled back, sending the monstrosity windmilling to the ground.

The severed head—still contained in a rusted helmet of its own—gazed up with green fire from the canyon floor, lipless teeth grinning as the jaw opened and closed, almost as if speaking.

As Doc stepped onto the back of the sled and Cipher revved the bike onto the trail once more, Deadeye gave the chattering skull a proper gridiron kick toward the two *draug* he'd left on the ground. It sailed into the fog and disappeared with a distant clank and clatter as it impacted the canyon wall.

He was about to turn away to rejoin his comrades when the unmistakable pinpoints of glowing emerald pierced the fog only yards away. One set, then two—the number he'd kept at bay.

Then three sets.

Four sets.

Green lights blinked on in the fog like sickly fireflies. Six, seven, eight pair.

A dozen.

The blood drained from Charlie's face and he began to back away from the twinkling wall of evil stars. He could hear Cipher and Doc calling to him from a hundred yards to the north. He heard the crunch of human footsteps in the frozen snow and knew the *draug* were moving toward him.

He recalled the loadout for the journey, and that part of the inventory was a case of fragmentation grenades. Patting down the front of his parka, he realized with a rising fear that he hadn't bothered to grab any for himself—they were safely in an ammo box on the sled.

Cipher pulled the Dugdale to a stop, looking back along the trail whence they'd come. The morning hung like a gauzy off-white curtain in the valley between the granite peaks.

Sound played tricks here, originating simultaneously from close by and echoing far away.

Doc stepped off the rear of the sled and peered into the blanket of arctic mist. "Charlie?" she shouted, hearing it played back to her from a hundred different locations. "Charlie!"

She could hear the rhythmic beat of footsteps on packed snow, and suddenly Deadeye appeared out of the fog, running at top speed. He was halfway past the bike and sled before he realized where he was, but immediately turned and fell on top of the sled, rummaging for a wooden crate painted olive drab with black stenciled text.

"Charlie, what are you—?" Doc started.

Before she could finish, the top of the box was off, and Deadeye had grabbed a small steel pineapple in each hand. "Keep going!" he barked, eyes widening as the curtain of green stars appeared again out of the fog.

Cipher revved the throttle again and the Dugdale took off, pulling the sled behind. Doc stepped on, her deeply worried face barely visible under the parka's fur-lined hood.

The green eyes grew silhouettes as they emerged from the mist. A full dozen undead Viking warriors, on the hunt for blood.

Deadeye scampered backward a good twenty yards in the crisp, dusty snow. Pulling the pin on the first grenade, he lobbed it toward the nearer canyon wall; the second he tossed directly into the center of the Viking mob.

Explosions echoed through the canyon, snow and ice joining a shower of rock, and once again everything went blank and white.

⊗

Jack had just secured the last exterior hatch when he heard the low rumble roll out of the canyon mouth. It sounded like a growl of thunder at first, although he knew there wasn't another storm due today. Grabbing two cups of coffee from the galley, he turned toward the engine room to see Sparks heading his way.

"Did you hear that too?" she asked.

Jack nodded, handing her a mug. "Yeah."

A moment passed as each sipped from their coffee and tried not to put their fears into words, lest they saddle the away party with some kind of self-made curse. It was bad enough they had to split up the crew. The sooner they patched up *Daedalus* and got her back in the air, the better.

Finally, Jack caught her brown eyes. "How you doing, Sparks?"

The engineer smiled. "I'm not exactly acclimated to the temperatures here," she said, putting on a stoic face. "Although I have been to Kilimanjaro, and visited the Tibesti Mountains in Chad. And I attended a diplomatic function in London with my father as a young girl—truly the coldest I've ever been before now."

They chuckled in unison.

"Here's to breaking new records," Jack offered, raising his coffee mug and sipping from it. "How's everything in the engine room?"

Sparks rubbed her eyes and went to the tiny galley sink, running some water into the now-empty mug and swishing it around. "The main power is back up, internal systems, radio and heat. We lost some gas in the crash before ballonet four was patched, and one of the helium reserve tanks was irreparably damaged. I can make it up in hydrogen. We'll just be a bit more combustible."

"If it means we can get some altitude and fly out of here," Jack mused, "I'm all for it." He downed the rest of his coffee in a single gulp and followed his mechanic's lead with his own mug. Tapping out the water into the sink, he left it hanging by its handle on a wall peg among the others. "What about restarting the thrusters if the turbofans are iced over?"

"I thought of that possibility. My new heating system is wired out to the thrusters as well. We just need to run it for about two hours before starting them." Sparks gave her captain a tired but competent wink.

"Well then," Jack chuckled, equally fatigued but plagued by the incessant worry of his away team's safety, "let's get to work unbending this bird."

- CHAPTER 11 -

Charlie gazed over the great wall of granite rubble and ice he'd made. Too late he'd realized this would close off their path back to the *Daedalus*. There was now no way back. Sparks and the captain would just have to come find them...eventually.

Making his way back to the motorcycle and sled, he informed Doc, Cipher, and Amaruq what had happened. Their return route no longer existed, but at least the *draug* were no longer an immediate threat.

They pushed on, out of the canyon and into another seemingly endless expanse of white tundra—a sprawl punctuated randomly by frozen columns of snow and ice. Northward they crawled, the whine of the motorcycle's dynamo the only sound for miles. Though mild, the wind was enough to disturb the top layer of loose powder from the ground, creating a three-foot layer of granulated mist across the landscape.

After just under four hours' travel, the sun dipped beneath the horizon and the sky went from hazy eggshell color to a dark purple, and the luminescent aurora came out to dance again in rippling bands of green, purple, and faded gold. The snowy landscape became a vast reflective surface for a host of bright stars and the shimmer of Northern Lights, creating a dazzling light box, despite the absence of the sun.

The group parked the Dugdale and sled in a semicircle under a rocky overhang, erecting a berm of snow to complete the shape and act as a wind stop. Cipher brought a cylindrical space heater about the size of an overnight bag out of the pile of supplies on the sled, connecting it to the Dugdale's dynamo. It brightened immediately, casting a soft orange glow over the interior of the rock wall, but Doc knew it would not be enough to keep them warm all night. A supplemental campfire was in order, but without any natural wood to be gathered, she was at a loss.

Amaruq smiled, using the moment to teach her compatriots some handy native survival skills. She took a cooking pot and made a fire with some lichen and seal fat, which Doc found most intriguing.

Cipher uncoupled the two halves of the field radio, crank-started the internal dynamo, and dialed in the comms frequency for the ship. "Away team to *Daedalus*," she addressed, "away team to *Daedalus*. We are safely encamped several miles north-northwest of the canyon exit. Weather clear. Expect to make good time tomorrow. Over."

After a brief crunch of static, Sparks replied over the headset: "Affirmative. Captain's outside, repairing the starboard envelope. Will inform when he returns. Over."

Cipher caught Doc's gesture from the corner of her eye and handed her the radio headset.

"Sparks?" Doc hailed into the microphone as she held the headset to her ear. "Tell Jack to get some sleep. Over." She passed the set back to Cipher, who heard the response: "Will do, Doctor. He's running on coffee and adrenaline, but he'll burn out soon. Stay safe. *Daedalus* out."

Then Cipher twisted the dial down to the lower frequencies where the alien signal had been picked up. She checked the chronometer on the field radio's control panel: 1959 hours. Her nimble fingers protruded through the "trap door" in the palm of the down mittens she'd been issued, deftly tuning the receiver.

As she watched the clock tick over to 2000 hours, a rhythmic pulse began to erupt from the earpiece. It followed the exact pattern that had been recorded, cataloged, parsed, and studied by all levels of AEGIS Intelligence. And, as it had done each time previously, the signal terminated in a pattern of electronic squelches and growls. Then the frequency went silent, except for the eerie background tone of solar winds in the atmosphere.

"Same?" Doc asked as she unscrewed a Thermos of hot cocoa.

"Same," Cipher nodded, folding up the radio and locking it shut.

The foursome set up a night watch of three hours each. Various cans of rations were opened and consumed, and everyone tried to settle in for a cold night as brilliant colors shifted across the sky.

The wind finally died, going completely still by 2100 hours.

At about 0200, as Amaruq was finishing her turn, the bears appeared.

"Charlie," Amaruq whispered, nodding toward the massive shape peering over the outcropping above the camp.

But Deadeye was already awake, alert, and had his Winchester trained on a second target, equally huge, shuffling around the north end of the snow berm. "No sudden moves," he instructed quietly, "but grab a weapon and be ready."

The huffing sounds of the apex predators' scent-gathering became audible above and beside the encampment. Doc and Cipher stirred awake, the latter cracking open the cylinder of a Webley field revolver with a muffled *click* under her thick mittens.

Deadeye watched along his gun sights until he was convinced all four of the party were on their feet. The massive shadow on which he was fixed hung back at the edge of the encampment, near the front of the Dugdale, horrifyingly still. Its eyes reflected blood red in the dim orange glow of the electric heater.

Charlie knew something of ursine behavior, having grown up around the black bears of rural North Carolina. They could often be frightened away by loud, sudden noises or distractions. On the other hand, he had no experience with the much larger bears of the polar variety. Cocking his head, he cast a quick glance toward Amaruq, deferring to her expertise.

The young woman crouched in a defensive squat, weight on her right leg, barbed harpoon low and aimed at the same shadow as Charlie's repeater.

A panicked cry arose from the camp, and all eyes turned toward Cipher. Her arm extended and she fired a shot with the Webley, intentionally wide of the giant silhouette by the motorcycle. The sound echoed through the curvature of the granite overhang, and the shadow charged.

As all four cast their attention on the lumbering form roaring toward them, another great shadow appeared over the camp. The second beast pounced from the rock shelf.

A flurry of tumbling violence erupted, the second predator clipping Cipher as it landed, lashing out with razor claws and gnashing teeth.

Doc rolled away, coming up in a crouch as the attacking beast rolled paws-over-snout, careening through the snow berm at the edge of camp.

Deadeye shifted the barrel of the Winchester toward the newcomer and fired, scoring a hit in the beast's front shoulder.

Cipher's pistol skittered through the hole in the berm and spun to a stop just feet from Amaruq.

Doc fired at the second polar bear as it crashed through the camp, and the first creature attacked from her left. Although the enchanted Greek vambrace she wore under her snow gear could have been of use, it had not been invoked, nor did she have time to do so.

Cipher staggered upright, dazedly scanning the campsite for her sidearm. Doc watched in horror as the giant ravening maw closed over Cipher's left shoulder, crushing it into a bloody mass. The beast shook its head from side to side, flipping its prey, doll-like. Then it suddenly let her go, hurling Cipher against the rock wall, where she collapsed in a heap of blood and shock.

The massive creature reared up on stocky hind legs, bellowing a feral war cry, fearsome claws brandished outward at its potential prey.

Doc emptied the cylinder of her .38 into the chest of the beast, just as a long, hooked spear appeared out of the night beyond her right shoulder. Amaruq's harpoon struck home in the creature's belly, and it roared again—this time in agony.

It clawed at the spear with savage paws the size of catchers' mitts, but the brutal barb kept it lodged in its gut. No longer able to stand upright, the snow-white behemoth fell forward, its own weight pushing the harpoon up through its abdomen and out the spine. It rolled and kicked in ferocious pain, spilling guts, spewing blood, slipping in its own warm viscera.

Deadeye racked shot after shot as the Winchester spat fiery lead at the second bear. With each cartridge spent, the marauding predator pounded forward on the snowy ground, Charlie tightening his aim. Then the beast was upon him, mouth full of dagger teeth ready to sink into his head. He felt a familiar pang of fear—a fear which gripped him from stem to stern and became a klaxon of impending doom.

Charlie Dalton inhaled the crisp Arctic air and shut his eyes. This was when the warrior was most alive, when standing upon the precipice of death.

At the last instant, the carbine's hot barrel pressed into the creature's brow and erupted in thunder.

The bear swayed on its massive legs momentarily, finally collapsing to the ground in a dead mass of bloodied white fur.

Deadeye lowered the carbine and took stock of the encampment. Amaruq had grabbed Cipher's pistol and approached the second bear, which was struggling wildly in its death throes. A shot rang out, and Amaruq pulled the Webley away from the bear's skull, barrel smoking. The creature lay still.

Doc knelt at Cipher's side, holding pressure on the grievous shoulder wound as blood seeped out over her gloves. The portable heater lay on its side, coils dark. Pieces of the field radio were scattered across the camp.

The cooking pot that had contained Amaruq's fire sat overturned, lodged in the snow.

Deadeye jogged to the rock wall under the overhang, Amaruq joining him at Doc's side.

"What do we do?" he asked.

Doc actually looked worried, and that scared Deadeye more than the obvious severity of Cipher's wound. She'd seen horrors beyond imagination, both in her time at the Western Front and in dealing with the occult megalomaniacs of the Silver Star, facing each without so much as a blink. If this worried She Who Was Unfazed, he knew it was bad indeed.

"We need to keep pressure on and get this bleeding stopped," Doc instructed. "I'll need to perform surgery, but there's no way I can do it here, under these conditions."

Amaruq turned and stepped away toward the sled, which had miraculously avoided any serious damage from the bear attack. She rummaged through her personal supplies for a few moments, then returned with an armload of things Deadeye could only guess at.

She dropped a field medical kit next to Doc, and for the first time noticed her wounded comrade's severe shivering and relative pallor. As Doc chattered instructions to Charlie, Amaruq began to concoct a poultice of various animal fats and mosses from her own kit.

"I need a shot of procaine, and the biggest bandages we have," said Doc, eyes beginning to redden with tears. Marissa was in rough shape. Doc wasn't sure if she could be stabilized.

"Use this over the wound before dressing it," Amaruq offered, hands full of yellowish, fatty, fibrous gel. "It will help the blood clot."

Doc hesitated a moment, then remembered how much indigenous wisdom had saved the lives of her crew over the past few years. She knew the properties of Amaruq's natural ingredients, and although they wouldn't necessarily save Cipher's life, it stood to reason they might help extend it until she could be operated on.

As Doc scooped a handful of the poultice and applied it over the brutal wound, Deadeye prepared the cotton bandages and a syringe of procaine as a local anesthetic. "This is great and all," he muttered, his voice unsure, "but how are we going to get her someplace you can actually perform surgery?"

No one was expecting the deep, masculine voice that echoed against the overhang in broken English.

"We maybe can help with that."

The party turned toward the shattered snow barrier, just beyond the carcass of the second polar bear, where stood a lone figure clad in white bear skins, and what appeared to be archaic leather armor and a fur-lined metal helm of clearly Viking design.

Deadeye stood to a defensive posture, pulling the Winchester to his hip, racking a cartridge into the chamber. "Hold up," he ordered. "Identify yourself."

The mysterious newcomer extended his arms from his sides, palms out. He was at least six feet tall, and muscular like a circus strongman. A bushy, copper beard sprouted from beneath the helmet, culminating in beaded braids above his chest.

As they watched, four additional figures appeared out of the darkened landscape, clad identically in white bear fur and ancient armor pieces. Three carried bows, with quivers of long arrows at the hip. The fourth, of a smaller, slighter frame, held an eight-foot spear. The three archers held their weapons at the ready, arrows nocked and ready for instant draw. The spear woman stalked far to the outside of the stranger's right flank.

As Deadeye held his rifle on the newcomers, Doc did some math, and the sum was disappointing. These were not the shambling mummies of the Golden City, or even the ravenous undead Inuit hunters they'd recently encountered. These were living people, well-adapted to the harsh environment and clearly competent at hunting dangerous predators.

Even with Deadeye's Winchester, Doc's .38 sidearm, and Amaruq's harpoon, there was no way to take them on and hope to win. Not with Cipher so badly wounded.

"It's okay, Charlie," Doc uttered softly, touching his shoulder as she stepped closer to him.

Slowly, Deadeye dropped the nose of the carbine.

A silent moment passed between the haggard explorers and the hunters who seemed to have stepped out of a Viking storybook. The archers remained absolutely still, neither raising nor lowering their weapons.

Amaruq stood, pulling the fur-lined parka hood to her shoulders, eyes wide with astonishment. "Sten?"

The man held position—not from cold, but a mind-numbing recognition. Slowly, he reached up and removed the ancient-looking helm, revealing a weather-tightened, red-cheeked face and mane of blond hair that shone in contrast to the fiery red beard. Liquid blue eyes squinted through the dark night, and his chapped lips pursed to speak the woman's name.

"Amaruq."

- CHAPTER 12 -

Jack was true to his word. The bent and sundered barrels of the twin Hotchkiss machine guns lay blackened and half-buried in the snow twenty yards away from their former home, alongside the remains of the powered gimbal and various pieces of the dorsal ball turret itself. Three hours with a socket wrench and two fragmentation grenades had done the trick.

Now, not only was the ship a couple of hundred pounds lighter, but nobody would be able to use the weapons against them.

The *Daedalus* remained anchored in place, vibrating every now and then under a slight buffet of wind. The strumming rhythms of Hoagy Carmichael's *Stardust* wafted from someplace within the silvery metal skin of the ship, guitars merging with piano, trumpet, and saxophone. The music was tinny and lacking any bass over the intercom speakers, but it was a welcome alternative to the whistle of Arctic weather outside.

Jack surveyed the gauges on the engine room control panel as all ten dynamos hummed in unison from the central generator bay. When he was satisfied that every internal system was nominal, he exited through the hatchway and climbed the aft ladder to the main gantry.

Running fore and aft like the spinal column of a whale, the catwalk was crowded on either side by the vulcanized canvas ballonets full of lift gas, previously compressed and sagging from the external temperature. Since the heating system had been brought back on line, however, the containment units were taut and full.

He joined Sparks midway down the gantry, where she crouched to repair a cracked brace that ran between the ballonets to the exterior skin.

"All systems check out," Jack announced. "Everything's jake."

The young engineer was facing away from him and didn't try to meet his gaze, but she nodded in the affirmative. "Good. We should be able to leave when I've made this last repair." She gestured behind her. "There's a pry bar leaning on the railing there. Can you help me?"

"Sure thing," said Jack. Taking the implement in hand, he moved next to Sparks, who instructed him where to wedge the bar. Jack followed her lead, awkwardly filling the silence with a nervous query. "What's it like," he asked as he leaned backward, pulling his weight on the pry bar, "to grow up in Kenya under British rule?"

Sparks peered through a pair of dark welding goggles, grasping the strut with one gloved hand, while holding the torch to the metal with the other. "Probably close to how Deadeye grew up under American rule," she said matter-of-factly. A shower of white-hot embers exploded from the point of her weld.

"Touché," Jack replied. "Although you know I didn't have any control over that..."

"No, of course not," Sparks shrugged, adjusting the torch and letting loose another shower of bright fire. "But you benefit from it just the same."

Jack continued pressing weight on the perforated beam by way of the crowbar. "True," he admitted. "I don't deny it. Just interested in your experience."

Sparks continued mending the previously-broken strut with several spot welds. "My experience? As a native Kikuyu in a British colony, I mattered little. As a Kikuyu *woman*, I mattered even less. But I was also the daughter of a chief. So, I used that small amount of status to go to school in Mombasa, with the assistance of the East Africa Women's League."

"I'm glad you did," Jack grunted, leaning against the bar with every ounce of strength he could muster.

Sparks put the final few welds on the strut, and gestured to Jack. "You can take the bar away," she instructed, pointing with a gloved hand. "I will give credit where it is due. The League advocated for me. But as the product of a colonial power, it was the least they could do."

"I understand," Jack said, wiping the sweat from his forehead with a bandanna from his trouser pocket. The heater was working well. "Europe sure did mess the bed in their handling of the war—and more besides—but I get the feeling that the days of empire are numbered. Ordinary folks are standing up to be counted."

Sparks pushed the welding goggles up onto her forehead. "That would be nice," she sighed, "but I'm not sure I share your optimism."

Jack suddenly thought of the disaffected souls across the globe, flocking to service in the Silver Star, and had to admit she had a point. "What still needs doing?"

Sparks cocked her head. "In regard to worldwide social inequity, or fixing the ship?"

"The ship," Jack chuckled. "We don't have the time or manpower for the other one."

"We need to run the engine heaters for a few hours, but all of the internal systems are optimal. I also rigged a couple of toggles on your helm panel to release the cables from inside the ship. We'll lose them, of course, but better than being outside in that cold, eh?"

"Wow! Excellent," laughed Jack. "Or dangling from the ladder as the ship flies away with nobody at the helm. Thank you! Turn on the engine heaters and hit the rack for four. You've more than earned some rest. I'll stay up and monitor the radio."

Sparks gave a casual two-fingered salute, and began to head toward the engine room.

"Oh, hey, Sparks?"

The mechanic paused and turned back to see Jack's face furrowed.

"Thanks for keeping her flying," he offered quietly, glancing around at the ship's interior. "Thanks…for everything,"

Approaching from his right, Sparks put her arms around his shoulders and gave her captain a friendly squeeze. It was something Rivets might have done, once upon a time. She flashed a half-smile as she passed behind him.

"Your heart is good," she said, disappearing down the corridor to the aft gantry ladder.

Jack leaned forward on the freshly-welded strut, firmly rubbing his eyes. "That would be nice," he muttered to himself, recalling the meat-grinder of the Western Front, "but I'm not sure I share your optimism."

⊗

A diffuse glow emanated from the air around the party, the sun having made its entrance for an ever-shortening day, light stretched like muslin over the landscape. The party pushed north and east across a snow-covered volcanic plain, Deadeye in the saddle of the electric motorcycle as it whirred through the crisp powder.

Cipher lay unconscious in the sidecar, bundled in a combination of her snow gear and a polar bear skin from the red-bearded Viking's personal stash.

The two ursine carcasses from the battle in the encampment were strapped onto the sled. Amaruq and Doc now sat astride two large, woolly caribou, flanked by the mysterious Norsemen on their own reindeer as they led the way through the blinding white. Their saddles were sturdily constructed of fur-trimmed leather, with stirrup treads of whale bone, and saddle horns to match, capped with the brass likenesses of polar bears. The animals themselves were all female, predominantly white with tawny markings, and among the larger specimens Doc had ever seen. Each possessed an impressive spread of antlers that sprouted like grasping skeletal claws from its head.

"Your English is quite good," said Doc as she goaded her mount in proximity to Sten's. "How did you learn?"

The burly man stared straight ahead, never taking his eyes from the snowy plain in the distance. "When I was of six years, a party of English explorers found our valley by accident. I learned from them."

Doc took in the information, searching her brain for any memory regarding a British expedition to the Arctic in the first decade of the century. The problem was that in the late Victorian and early Edwardian period, British expeditions of discovery were as common as pebbles on a beach, and many of them simply disappeared. "What happened to them?" she asked.

Sten continued in his forward gaze. "They stayed among us for two summers, learning our ways and teaching us of the outside world. They left during a bad storm. One of our hunting parties found their bodies in the Northeast Pass the following spring. The Goðar Council called it punishment for the corruption of our traditions and culture."

"The *Goðar*?"

"A *Goði* is a...priest. All the *Goðar* sit on a ruling council."

"So you have no king, or chieftain?"

"My father is king. But the *Goðar* hold much sway over the people."

"And how is it that your people came to be here?"

"We are descended from explorers who came with Erik Thorvaldsson."

Doc blinked at the mention of the name. "Erik Thorv...do you mean Erik the Red?"

"Even he." Sten sat up straight in his saddle, chest forward.

Amaruq brought her mount in line with Sten's, opposite Doc. "Are you sure it will be alright to bring us into your valley?" she asked. "If the *Goðar* prohibit outsiders..."

For the first time, Sten glanced to his left and saw the Hammer of Thor pendant he'd given Amaruq fifteen years ago, a badge of sorts, for safe passage. It hung on a thong of caribou hide, protruding from her parka hood and plunging down to mid-chest.

"I am the king's son," he said. "You are my guests. One of yours requires a healer's services, and you have brought two white bears as a gift. If the people have full bellies, they will be content. And if they are content, the *Goðar* will not interfere." He turned his attention back toward their northeasterly course through the snow. "I see you kept the hammer."

Amaruq blushed beneath the fur hood. "Of course I kept it," she said softly. "You saved our lives, mine and Anarsi's."

The Viking's face softened at the memory. "And how fares Anarsi?"

Amaruq's head dropped as she stifled a tear. "He was...killed. He...he became a *draug*."

Sten suddenly locked up, his jaw set forward. "When did this happen?" he asked with gravel in his tone.

"Two days ago."

"The dead have been restless for several days," Sten explained.

Amaruq gasped. "You have encountered the *draug*?"

"As I said, the dead have been...restless."

The party continued on in silence for a few moments. Then: "I'm sorry your uncle challenged our hunting party," Sten offered. "He need not have died."

Amaruq nodded in understanding. "He pushed us north of the pass. It was not our territory."

There was a long, silent pause, then Sten regarded Amaruq for the second time in as many minutes. "And why are you north of the pass this time?"

"I'm working with Doctor Starr and the others."

Sten turned his gaze toward Doc. "You are explorers? Like the English?"

Doc had been content to piece together the story from their conversation, but now she was on the spot. "N-not exactly," she stammered. "We are part of an international..." Doc paused, realizing that members of an isolated culture would have no idea as to how small the world had become merely over the past century. "It's a large group, from many nations. We fight evil magic." She smiled to herself, confident that even a Viking a thousand years out of time would be able to grasp the concept.

"Like the *draug*?" Sten asked.

Doc smiled. "Among other things."

"Tell me."

As the party trudged along their icy path, Doc revealed the mission of AEGIS, along with a descriptive profile of Aleister Crowley's *Astrum Argentum*, and some of her crew's experiences tangling with their agents. She told Sten about closing the demonic portal in the Amazon, of their encounter in the Himalayas, their battle in the Egyptian desert, and the trek across the Pacific Ocean to defend a race of beast-folk from Silver Star occupation. She talked about the harrowing aerial adventures they'd had aboard the *Daedalus*, and the exotic places they'd visited.

Finally, she explained their current mission: investigate the mysterious alien signal, retrieve whatever was sending it, and do it all before the Silver Star could grab it.

Amaruq nodded occasionally, confirming what she could with her own knowledge.

To his credit—and Doc's utter surprise—Sten took everything in stride, nodding acknowledgments as she spoke, asking for clarifications when necessary. Doc had been so intent on the conversation that she hadn't noticed the passage of four long hours of travel.

As the party crested a small, snow-capped rise, they looked out onto a short stretch of flat, white tundra much like they'd been crossing. But beyond it rose a fortress of gray mountains streaked with snow, towering into the low clouds.

Cruel winds whipped the snow and ice around the mountains into innumerable cyclones, creating a hazardous gate of foul weather in front of the southern entrance.

Doc stood tall in her caribou saddle, gobsmacked. She realized they were about to cross a large body of frozen water of some kind. Had they made it to the coast already?

"Is that the pass?" Amaruq asked.

Sten nodded as the rest of his party drew up in a line on the small rise. "And beyond lies *Bålgard.*"

Doc turned toward him. "*Bålgard*? Is that..."

"Our valley," Sten replied, dismounting his reindeer and retrieving a long coil of rope from the saddle. "Come on."

Sten gestured to his fellow Vikings, barking commands in Old Norse. With his mount in the lead, the caribou riders attached their own to the rope and ambled forward single-file, Deadeye taking up the rear on the Dugdale.

They pressed toward the strange canyon in a single line across the ice, and within twenty minutes, had disappeared into the roiling miniature storm.

- CHAPTER 13 -

Jack sat slumped in the pilot's station on the *Daedalus* bridge, watching the snow and ice shift across the windscreen like a child's kaleidoscope. The clock on the control panel told him the heaters still had to run another hour before takeoff would be possible. He wasn't used to simply waiting around, and he didn't like the experience. Not with Doc and the away party out there on their own.

When Sparks stepped across the hatch threshold onto the bridge, the distraction was welcome.

"Systems check, results optimal," she announced. "Heaters are running and we can attempt takeoff in—"

"In about an hour?" Jack finished her sentence, continuing to stare out at the snow blowing across the forward window array.

"So you *are* keeping track," Sparks smiled.

Suddenly a hiss of static broke over the bridge speakers, and Jack spun in the pilot's seat to face the radio console. They both froze in place, absolutely still, straining to hear the next sound. It came in a distorted rush of pilot chatter, most of it in German.

Sparks cast an expectant glance at Jack, not understanding the words spoken, but interpreting the situation via her captain's reaction.

His next statement was softly spoken, but sent a chill of fear rocketing up her spine where it coiled at the nape of her neck.

"Silver Star. They've found us."

Sparks' eyes grew wide. "Found *us*, or the away party?"

"*Us.* They've located the *Daedalus*." Jack turned forward to the control panel and began flipping switches.

Sparks remained stuck in place, unsure of her next words or actions. Then she realized Jack was powering up the external engines. "The heaters haven't had enough time—"

"We can't stay here," Jack growled. He paused a moment, swiveling back around to lock eyes with his engineer. "Sparks, I know since you signed on, I've asked a lot of you. And you've never let me down. But I'm going to need more, if we expect to get out of here in one piece."

Another burst of static and a quick pilot exchange from the radio speakers told Jack their time was running out. Silver Star airships were colossal and usually carried a small squadron of four to six planes, and their pilots were attentive and methodical. If their search protocol from the Himalayas held true, one or two would be on their location soon.

Sparks took a deep breath and nodded. "What should I do?"

"I need to fly *Daedalus* out of here," Jack began, "but I need eyes up top."

Sparks almost gave an audible gasp as she realized what he wanted her to do. "You realize the dorsal turret is gone?"

Jack sighed. "I know it's a lot, but I can only fire the forward machine guns straight ahead. I need you to keep the bad guys off our back. If that means cabling you to the ladder and sticking a Tommy gun out the top hatch, we have to do it."

Her stomach began to tie itself in knots, and Sparks felt the bile rise in her throat. But the simplistic way in which Jack had put their predicament was reminiscent of an excited schoolboy going to his local cinema to watch the latest serial, and a sudden calm washed over her.

Shaking off the fear and preliminary nausea, she gave a casual salute to her chief and nodded. "Aye, Captain. I'll figure it out."

Then she was gone, and Jack could hear her boots on the aluminum rungs of the ladder leading topside. "I know you will," he answered softly to himself. He scanned the control console for his engine toggles and, mouthing a quick and distinctly non-Catholic "Hail Mary", switched each one on in sequence.

The port-side engines had more direct exposure to the weather, and the aft one took its sweet time starting up. Jack toggled it on and off a few times to jar the fan blades loose from the mass of ice encrusting them. When he was satisfied all four lateral thrust engines were generating satisfactory RPMs, he turned his attention to the massive thruster on each side.

Switching on the power to the starboard thruster, he heard the ice break apart and the turbofan slowly cycle up. Next to the starboard thruster power control lay the port thruster switch. Jack toggled it on, listening as the electric whine built toward what he knew would either be a short in the power circuit or freedom from the ground.

"Damn," he muttered, switching the power down before toggling on again. This time, he heard the telltale crack of ice shattering as the fan blades revved up. With a satisfied sigh, he donned the somewhat cumbersome communications headset and pushed the *TALK* button on the console. "Okay, all engines online and giving optimal revs. What's your status?"

Sparks stood on the perforated metal steps of the ladder, just below the dorsal hatch. She was already uncomfortably bundled in her field parka and a black knit balaclava, a freshly-loaded Thompson submachine gun dangling heavily at the shoulder strap. Unable to wear snow gloves with full coverage on her trigger hand, she'd opted for a wool mitt with half fingers.

She pulled her goggles down over her eyes, an amber crescent from the gantry lights reflecting off each lens, and plugged her headset patch cord into a panel in the ceiling adjacent to the hatch. "I'm getting set topside," she answered. "Not cabled in yet, but if you have to fly, go ahead."

Jack unplugged his headset cable and went to the comms console, flipping a couple of switches that had the effect of opening a shipwide channel. Then he returned to the pilot's seat and strapped in. Despite the sub-zero temperature outside the ship, the interior heaters were functioning at peak performance, and he'd shed his uniform jacket, leaving it in the locker between the bridge and main saloon. Pushing the sleeves of his thermal undershirt to his elbows, he secured his harness and gripped the flight control yoke. He fished the audio plug from the end of the headset wire and stuck it back into the console. Within a couple of seconds, he'd unwrapped a stick of licorice chewing gum and crammed it into his mouth. Suddenly, another garish blast of radio chatter on the Silver Star frequency told Jack the Silver Star had made visual contact. They had to leave now.

"Detaching cables," he warned, "in three...two...one."

As he flipped each of the two toggles on the console in turn, the exterior cleats snapped open, allowing the cables to release and simple physics lift the *Daedalus* gently into the air.

The ship was immediately hammered and jostled by cold northerly winds, and Jack had to fight the yoke to keep from being slammed into the cliffside once again. Fortunately they were far lighter now than when they'd crashed.

Sparks gripped the handle to the lateral locking bar, levering open the hatch. The wind shear pushed it over, out of her hands and onto the dorsal surface with a loud *clang*. Climbing another couple of rungs up the ladder, she positioned herself at waist height in the hatchway and locked a carabiner from her safety harness onto the hook outside the opening. She reached toward the hatch door and, with the twist of another lever, locked it into the brackets that kept it in the open position.

Wind and ice blasted her face, gathering in small layers around her shoulders. Clearly the concept of "daylight" in northern Greenland in September was a gauzy whitewash, but at least Sparks would be able to see anyone coming. As she waited and watched from the top hatch, the ship continued to rise into the strengthening storm.

She heard another burst of static over the headset, and within seconds the black silhouettes of two Heinkel HD 23 fighter planes banked out of the milky sky and roared down on them. "Two fighters, hot on our six!" Sparks cried into the headset.

Jack angled the flight yoke to starboard and throttled all the way up, leaving the icy confines of the canyon behind. He felt the ship's envelope shudder with wind and the impact of gunfire, and he hauled back on the controls, climbing with full power into the savage sky.

○R

The pass was narrow, perhaps only twenty feet wide, and the wind blasted through at what felt like hurricane force. Visibility was next to zero, and Doc hugged her parka closely around her body as her mount strode calmly and surely through the tempest. She marveled at the nonchalance and tenacity of the native caribou, a duality of nature well-suited to their extreme environment.

Not a word was spoken, for the simple reason that no sound was audible above the raging Arctic wind through the canyon. And it wasn't merely wind; it was every manner and form of water, from liquid to solid, carried on its cold wings. Everything from curling mist to razor-sharp ice shards was represented, and several times Doc caught herself fearing no end to their passage.

This could very well be a ruse to lure the already exhausted party into the mountains and murder them. It would be an easy matter to stash their bodies somewhere out of plain sight, but still exposed to the bitter cold. They'd be ice-encrusted skeletons in a matter of weeks or days—unless the mysterious radio pulse brought them back as mindless, ravenous *draug*.

As the minutes became an hour, Doc came to realize what an incredible natural barrier the canyon was. Not just the passage itself, with its constant torrent of icy wind, but the surrounding mountains which reached up to disappear in the thick clouds above. Despite much of Greenland being a flat, desolate, snowy expanse, she knew some of its mountain ranges could hit ten or twelve thousand feet.

Doc continued to make a variety of calculations in her head: estimating the distance traveled through the pass; the possible source of the storm winds focused through it; the possible height of the surrounding mountain peaks. There was a brief moment when the wind subsided, and Doc looked upward to see a scoop-like formation in the rock that literally funneled extreme wind out of the weather systems above and shot it down the pass.

As they continued on, it was as if a curtain had drawn back and they were finally past the security gate.

Then they were through.

Sten emerged first on his giant, shaggy mount, followed by the other riders, squinting away from the diffuse brightness of the sky above them.

Beyond the trail on which they traveled lay a sprawling green valley, dotted with cultivated farmland and alpine meadows, crisscrossed by babbling creeks of fresh water. It lay cradled between the white mountain peaks, perhaps four miles long and as many wide—lush, verdant real estate in the middle of a frozen wasteland.

A thick forest range of evergreens stretched toward the opposite end, the likely source of timber for the various homes and structures built in distinctive 10th century Nordic style.

Doc's jaw dropped open as she surveyed the scene before her, pushing her snow goggles to her forehead. Men and women of Norse extraction tilled fields, harvested crops, and gathered fish traps from the brooks and shallow river eddies. Children herded goats and played with dogs, throwing sticks to chase in the open meadows. They wore simple homespun clothing of a bygone era, and cultivated generally long hair, often braided in some fashion. For the first time, she noticed how comparatively, unexpectedly warm it had suddenly become.

Taking down her hood and doffing her parka altogether, she saw that a series of thermal geysers ringed the entire valley, creating a life-sustaining habitat for what was apparently a few hundred healthy and productive members of their society.

Somewhere in the distance, a bell rang. It was answered by the low bellow of a horn.

All eyes gradually shifted their way as they left the canyon trail and continued in toward the center of the valley on a well-maintained gravel path. Doc and Amaruq exchanged a suspicious look, then Deadeye caught their attention, nodding toward an approaching group of serious-looking men and women. She followed his indication and realized they were about to either be welcomed with open arms or be brutally executed, and Doc wasn't laying odds on which was more likely.

As the welcoming committee approached, Charlie immediately took a visual inventory. A single man led the column of five women, each carrying a round wooden shield and a seven-foot iron-tipped spear.

The man in front had a braided beard of platinum blond tinged with white, and locks to match. He wore an embroidered tunic and leather trousers. An ornately-tooled leather scabbard hung at his hip, the exquisitely-crafted antique sword housed within.

Charlie pulled to a stop on the Dugdale, hidden behind the caribou riders at the front. Reaching back, he silently pulled the Winchester repeater from its sling behind the saddle, resting it on his lap. He cast a glance downward, noting Cipher was still unconscious in the sidecar. Her breathing was shallow, and what he could see of her face was pale and gaunt. He hoped these officials would let them pass and allow Doc to perform surgery to save Cipher's life.

But then the man in front barked something in Old Norse, and the spears came down, leveled at the party. Sten held up a hand in protest, yelling back at the man in his own language. The reindeer startled and began to stomp the ground, reins tugging, their riders scolding.

"Aww hell," Charlie muttered. "I guess it's gonna get ugly."

- CHAPTER 14 -

Sparks braced herself in the hatch opening, boots lodged firmly in the ladder rungs. Her stomach plunged with the rise of the bleak horizon, and suddenly she was gazing directly at the incoming fighter planes. Despite the warmth of the balaclava, her nose and cheeks felt frozen as all the blood drained away from her face in fear. Setting her back against the rim of the hatch portal, she gripped the Tommy with both hands, took a rough approximation of aim, and squeezed the trigger.

Dhakiya Kitur had fired small arms in the past, but nothing like the bucking bronco that was the Thompson. It roared and kicked, spitting hot .45 caliber rounds into the sky. She huffed and winced as her shoulder took the pounding of the recoil. Without tracers to help guide her fire, most of the burst went wide, lost to the icy winds.

The first fighter came in from below, lighting a trail of incendiary fire up the spine of the climbing airship. Sparks could tell the envelope had been re-damaged, and they would be losing lift gas again as a result. In a rage, she opened up into the belly of the plane as it climbed, clipping the fuel line and rupturing a seam in the underside of the pilot compartment, which suddenly erupted in flame.

As the fighter banked away in a high wingover, its engine stalled, and it plummeted to the ground, trailing fire and smoke.

The second fighter came in for its pass, but took a stray wind current and lost its aim. Green tracers flew randomly wide of its climbing target. The plane shot past, climbing into a turn to come around at the unprotected belly of the *Daedalus*. Banking over to its left, the fighter completed the one-eighty and prepared to attack at full throttle.

But the *Daedalus* had disappeared.

In point of fact, her expert pilot had found a cloud bank large enough to hide within, cutting the powerful turbofans to allow the airship to drift along with it.

Taking a much wider berth, the plane cut throttle and began a methodical probe of the surrounding clouds and fog. Soon, the drone of its engines could no longer be heard over the whistle of Arctic wind.

Sparks felt her stomach settle as the ship leveled off.

"Okay, Sparks, come below," Jack ordered, his low tone crackling over Dhakiya's headset.

"Stand by. Need to check for leaks," she replied. "Took some hits to the outer envelope."

"Affirmative."

Sparks clambered down the forward access ladder, grunting in pain with every rung. She was sure her shoulder would be bruised for some time. Trudging from fore to aft and back again, she made a visual inspection of each of the twelve rubberized canvas containment bags, noting at least three bullet impacts in the struts and floor panels that had miraculously flown clear of the precious ballonets.

On her way forward, she spied a small hole in ballonet two, whistling with escaping helium-hydrogen compound. She retrieved the repair kit stored midway back on the starboard side, flipping open the aluminum lid and rummaging for a patch and the jar of rubbery liquid adhesive. Before another thirty seconds had passed, the breach had been sealed, and Sparks headed for the forward gantry ladder.

She stepped onto the bridge and saw Jack turn in the pilot's seat, jawing a stick of licorice gum with a grin.

"Nice work, lady," he winked.

Sparks leaned against the doorway and smiled painfully. "I shot a plane out of the sky. With this little thing." Tapping the stock of the Thompson with a nearly frozen finger, she set it in the corner and went to the radio station to flop down in the chair.

"Yes, you did," Jack chuckled. "Welcome to the improbable club."

Sparks laughed back. Suddenly, there was a burst of static over the radio, and both could hear an exchange between the Silver Star pilot and its headquarters.

"Better get a radio detector reading," Jack suggested, "make sure that fighter's really gone."

But Sparks was already fitting the radio console headset over her ears. "Way ahead of you, Captain.

With the flip of a switch, she powered up the detector and began narrowing the band. The familiar *deet-deet-deet-deet* of radio waves spreading outward in ever widening rings pierced the bridge. She saw a shape appear on the round view screen and let out an audible gasp.

"Talk to me, Sparks. What've you got?"

"I'm...not sure."

"Is it the other fighter?"

"No sir," came the reply. "Bigger...*much* bigger."

Jack adjusted as a sudden tailwind nudged the ship forward. He allowed a soft laugh to himself. *Of course it's bigger,* he thought. *It's one of the Silver Star's supercarriers. The* Luftpanzer II *or the* Osiris...*or another one entirely.* "Where away?" he asked.

"About forty miles north-northeast on our present course. It's moving slowly on a westerly heading."

"Any sign of the fighter?"

"Yes sir. It seems to be heading toward the larger craft."

"Well," Jack said, all-business. "We know where the Silver Star is, and where they're going. We know that *they* know we're poking around too."

"I don't feel good about this, Captain," Sparks sighed, watching the back of Jack's head with nervous tension. "They have so many troops and resources..."

"It's okay, Sparks," Jack assured. "We've got two things in our favor: agility, and that radio detector for seeing where they are."

As he spoke, and Sparks returned her gaze to the small glass screen, the enormous shape vanished from sight.

"Um, sir?" Sparks stammered, twisting the dial in an attempt to better focus the signal. "We might have a problem."

◊

Sten repeated his address to the leader of the guards, and the spears receded to a more respectful distance. Doc watched the exchange as she simultaneously tried to keep her reindeer mount calm.

The leader paused a moment, taking in the party with a glance, then barked an order at the guardswomen. He turned on his heel and retreated toward the gargantuan meeting hall at the center of the valley. The soldiers again turned their attention, and their spears, to the party, motioning them to an area of stables and timber huts near the hall.

Deadeye didn't relish the thought of going deeper into the lion's den if they were going to have to fight their way out, but he couldn't argue that Cipher needed surgical help, and fast, if she were to survive. Revving the snowcycle forward at pace with the caribou, he made visual note of all the best places to hide or find cover.

As they moved slowly through the valley, toward its center full of homes and public facilities, Doc thought it felt rather like going back in time to the age of the real Vikings. Here was an enclave of people insulated from the outside world, unchanged for a thousand years.

They spoke Old Norse and kept the same fashion, technology, and traditions as their forbears some thirty generations distant. If she didn't have a patient badly in need of her surgical skill, she could see spending years here, studying the people and their society. This was a treasure trove of historical and cultural data here for even the most casually curious anthropologist.

At first, the Dugdale passed without much notice. But when people began to realize it was moving under its own power and not being pulled by one of the reindeer, a crowd began to form. The mass of bystanders kept pace with the party as they were led along a grass-lined alpine path deep into the valley.

With every few yards' progress, another handful of curious Norsefolk would leave their farming tasks and join the group of onlookers. Deadeye kept the Winchester sideways across his lap, an easy grab with his throttle hand.

Eventually they were brought to a halt outside several reindeer pens, where they were told to dismount and wait in a public dwelling used as a staging structure for ceremonial purposes. As various men- and women-at-arms unloaded the mounts and secured them in the pens, Amaruq and Doc gingerly lifted Cipher from the motorcycle sidecar and carried her into the building.

The windowless structure was rustic but not uncomfortable, constructed of a timber and stone frame, with a ceiling of latticed pine branches, and covered in mossy turf on the exterior. A central hearth and chimney made of stone pierced the ceiling, fire already crackling within. Woven mats and furs covered the dirt floor.

"I am sorry," Sten sighed as Doc and Amaruq carried Cipher to a bed of stretched fiber cord and piled furs. "The *Goðar* have no patience for outsiders since the English came those years ago."

"I just hope we're not too late to save Cipher," Doc worried. She rummaged through their supplies left inside the structure, locating her surgical bag and returning to her patient's bedside. Rolling out the collection of medical instruments, she waved Amaruq over to help. "Can you hold the light for me?"

Amaruq nodded, grabbing one of the surviving camp lanterns and moving next to Doc.

Sten followed with, "You have my protection." He shared a lingering, silent gaze with Amaruq. He then retreated to the opposite end of the home with his fellow hunters, speaking Old Norse in hushed tones.

Charlie took up a sentry position by the door, eyes roaming from the cluster of Viking hunters in one half of the house to Doc's primitive surgical theater in the other.

"Okay, Cipher," Doc whispered. "Let's get you fixed up."

○R

The sun was already long past its apex when a local Viking, a tall, middle-aged man with a copper beard, who clearly knew Sten quite well, entered the structure and went directly to speak with him.

Cipher lay still, in deep sleep, her wound repaired to the best of Doc's ability given their present resources. Her shoulder was wrapped in fresh cotton bandages—the last in the supply kit—over another mossy poultice of Amaruq's construction. Doc sat close by, keeping alert for any signs of fever or infection.

Deadeye stood in the much the same position that he'd been in two hours ago. He gripped the walnut stock of the Winchester carbine, wondering why the valley guardians had let any of them keep their weapons. Eventually he figured it must have had something to do with their intricate rules around hospitality and left it at that.

Amaruq sat on a pile of furs near the fire hearth, listening with interest to the discussion between the two tall Viking men. She spoke passable Danish, but the Old Norse these two conversed in was a step beyond anything she was familiar with.

Still, the occasional word would fall from their sentences like a penny accidentally dropped on a seaside boardwalk. She watched as Sten absorbed the full weight of what this messenger was telling him, their eyes growing wide together as she realized what it was all about.

Sten gripped the man by his shoulders and huffed through clenched teeth, thanking him for the news but clearly disturbed by the contents of it. Then the messenger was gone, and Sten approached the crew opposite the hearth. "My cousin Halfdan says the *Goðar* have decided you are to be killed."

Deadeye's hands tensed on the gun stock, and Doc rose like a shot.

"What?!" she demanded.

"Sacrificed," Sten replied, "to *Freyja*."

"And what of you?" Amaruq asked quietly from the stone fireplace.

Sten's brow furrowed in the dim light. "Because of my status, we will...not be."

"Fantastic," Deadeye scowled.

"I swear to you," Sten boomed, his solemn presence filling the open room, "that you will not suffer this fate."

Doc was a statue, tight-lipped and surgical in her words. "I swear to *you*, we have no intention to."

Once again, Amaruq and Sten locked eyes in an unspoken exchange that said more than any words could. The look of fear on the Inuit woman's face struck the Viking's heart, and he visibly winced. He'd saved her life years ago. He would not allow that life to be taken now. Not without a fight. Even if it meant slaughtering every last *Goðar* in the valley.

"So what's the plan?" Deadeye mused, clutching the rifle to his chest.

Doc flew into motion. "Get our supplies packed up and ready by the door," she ordered, pulling the revolver from its canvas holster at her hip and flicking the cylinder open. "Sten, seeing as how there aren't any windows in this hut, can one of your hunters stand outside and relay the situation as it happens?"

Sten puzzled at the syntax of her words, but got the basic gist of what she wanted. He growled something in Old Norse, and one of the hunters stepped forward, bow in hand. The Viking leader waved a hand, and the hunter disappeared through the door.

Doc wrung her hands together. "Charlie, do you think the field radio can be repaired to get a brief signal out?"

"I dunno," he worried, shaking his head. "The bears tore it up something fierce. It's in pieces."

Doc cast a soft look at her friend and comrade. "Can you try?"

"Yes ma'am."

Leaning his rifle next to the door, Charlie went to the hide-covered bundle of electronic parts and began pawing through the contents. He'd built his share of primitive crystal radio sets in the past, but he wasn't altogether sure he'd find enough functioning parts among this carnage to make anything worthwhile. First he'd need a power source. The field radio's dynamo was damaged beyond easy repair, but there were three flashlights among their gear, each containing two carbon-zinc D-cell batteries.

It was a start.

Kneeling by the hearth, Deadeye went to work connecting and disconnecting, spooling and unspooling, performing the electronic version of the surgery Doc had done to save Cipher. Within a few short minutes, he'd Frankensteined a working transmitter and tuning coil, and cannibalized enough spare wire to fashion a makeshift antenna and ground. The telegraph key and headset were still attached to the front of the box, and functional.

He stood from the hearth, offering the headphones. "There ya go, Doc. Give 'er a whirl."

"I knew you could do it." Doc allowed herself the flash of a grateful smile, taking the headphones and kneeling down by the chaotic assemblage of radio parts. Cradling the headset to her left ear, she tapped out a brief signal in Morse code on the telegraph key, then switched off the radio. "For all the good it'll do…"

The hunter returned from outside, relaying something to Sten in a rush of incomprehensible words.

"*Já*," Sten nodded, turning to look at his new friends. "The *Goðar* have sent warriors for us. We are to come with you to the execution place."

Deadeye picked up the Winchester and racked the lever. "What about Cipher?"

"We need to buy some time," Doc fumed, pacing the mats on the floor. "Just to get her back in the sidecar, so that—" She halted in mid-stride. "What the hell...?"

The dull thud of an explosion rumbled in from far outside the village center. It was followed by the staccato beat of automatic weapons, and the entire town suddenly erupted in chaos.

Deadeye cracked the heavy door open and peered out. The denizens of the valley ran to and fro with purpose, clutching weapons to fight with or valuables to hide. Unable to see anything worthwhile from this vantage, he pushed through the door and scrambled onto the low, sloping roof, hefting the Winchester up first and following it with tenacious hands and feet.

He stood atop the turf that covered the house and made his way to the central chimney, grabbing the rifle from the roof as he went. From the peak of the roof line, he had an impressive view of the valley, the village structures close by, the creeks and tributaries, the fields and farms. As he peered past the main hall in the center of the village, he saw them: a dozen soldiers in modern snow camouflage fatigues and parkas, carrying Fedorov Avtomat rifles with white-painted stocks. He hadn't seen that type of long arm at the Western Front, but he knew it to be a Russian-made gun. He also knew the Silver Star had friendly ports in the Baltic.

It occurred to him that these could very well be Russian cohorts, or mercenaries at the very least. Regardless of their status within the *Astrum Argentum*, they were well-armed and equipped, approaching from the north end of the valley, and slaughtering indiscriminately as they came.

Deadeye turned, glancing behind him at the south entrance to valley, from the direction his own party had come. They were just about dead center within the alpine oasis, making a two-mile approach from either end a dicey prospect at best—which made the Russians' incursion to the central valley all the more impressive to Charlie.

Everywhere beyond the mountains that ringed this little temperate Eden seemed to be under white-out conditions, dark storm clouds roiling and shuddering in the distance, yet the sky directly overhead was mild and overcast. Scanning the gravel path below, he saw that the Dugdale remained parked next to the house, unmolested.

Taking up a position with the chimney as cover, Deadeye knelt atop the sod roof, kicking a small hole in it with his boot heel. "Looks like a dozen paramilitary. Maybe Silver Star, possibly…Russians?" he called down through the breach.

"Any sign of Jack?" Doc shouted back.

"Negative," Deadeye answered. "Enemy's encroaching from the north. I'm gonna stay up here and cover you. Let you know when to get Cipher out of the house. Meantime stay put."

As he watched the Russian agents approach, two fell with Viking arrows protruding from white-clad torsos. *Good shooting, you guys,* he thought to himself. When he knew they were pulling within effective range of the Winchester's two-hundred yards, he raised it to his shoulder and sighted down the barrel.

The rifle spat fire and smoke, and a third gunman toppled over like a spilled grocery bag. Still the white-clad agents pressed forward, leaping piled stone fences and using livestock as cover. The rattle of their own rifles echoed through the valley, and Deadeye could see the lifeless bodies of men, women, and children fall in the fields and along the paths.

These were indiscriminate killers, most likely under orders to capture or eliminate the *Daedalus* crew—who, if the carrier vessel had overheard Doc's wireless message, knew were in the valley somewhere.

Deadeye did some quick calculations in his head. The Dugdale was never a fast motorcycle, but in its current snow configuration, was even slower. Not an especially agile getaway vehicle on gravel paths. A reindeer mount was the more nimble option, but even if they strapped Cipher tightly to the beast, the potential jostling could negatively impact Doc's expert surgery. If the Russians made it within the village and managed to torch the sod roof of their tiny fortress in the middle of town, there was only one door and no windows. Certain death one way or another if they stayed. It would have to be the Dugdale, and a steadfast hope that Captain Stratosphere would reach them with the *Daedalus* in time.

"Get ready to move Cipher to the motorcycle when I give the word," he ordered.

Sten emerged from the house and Deadeye watched as he disbursed his hunters to the front lines to defend their valley. The copper-bearded Viking stabbed a half dozen arrows into the ground next to the Dugdale, then bent a bow of mountain ash across his right thigh, stringing it in a single, well-practiced motion.

As the invaders pressed further into the valley, Deadeye made out the lumbering form of a machine-gun crew laden with ammo drums, the lead man with a Russian-made DP-28 slung across his shoulder like a baseball bat. These Silver Star cohorts had managed a foothold at the north end of the valley, and would continue to press on unless given a decisive bloody nose—and perhaps not even then.

For the first time, Deadeye realized that the fallen agents had not begun to simmer and melt away in tendrils of black smoke as was customary for acolytes of the *Astrum Argentum*. These were men who had either refused the blood pact of the Silver Star, or were simply mercenaries and not "true believers", as Doc called the rank and file. The latter possibility actually provided a chance of scaring them off with a show of force, whereas Silver Star regulars would continue to fight to the last with nothing to lose.

Turning to look back the way they'd come, to the valley entrance in the south, he saw a bullet-shaped shadow fall across the meadow, and knew he'd have to time this right.

"Doc!" Deadeye cried through the hole in the roof. "Enemy has a machine gun. You get Cipher in the Dugdale and get ready to ride. I'll take Sten to cover the escape. *Daedalus* inbound—repeat: *Daedalus* inbound!"

- CHAPTER 15 -

Deadeye knew the range on most light machine guns was somewhere in the neighborhood of eight hundred yards. Easily four times his Winchester, and many times more than Sten's simple hunting bow. They weren't equipped to take on such a nimble and devastating weapon in a fair fight. They would have to keep out of the DP-28's line of fire, unless they could draw it away from the *Daedalus* as she came in for a quick landing to pick up her crew.

Heading toward the approaching Russians at a fast jog, the two men crossed the main road through the settlement to a large timber structure on the east side, which appeared to be a blacksmith shop and livery for the domesticated caribou, in Deadeye's estimation.

Flattening himself against the exterior wall, Deadeye peered into the distance, noting a small squad of mercenaries working their way up to the outskirts of the town. "Keep an eye on them," he pointed to Sten, who nodded solemnly and ducked inside the building.

Before Deadeye could question his Viking ally, Sten had cleared the interior ladder and was waving down from the hayloft window. Across the grazing meadow, a mercenary crouched, taking aim with his FA rifle at a small unit of Viking warrior women engaged in a standoff with four Russians by the shore of a lake, some three hundred yards distant. While he couldn't hope to hit the targets at the lake, he could split the difference to the meadow and—*crack!*—the Winchester boomed, the shot echoing across the valley. The gunman in the meadow dropped in place, unmoving.

Suddenly a cry rang out from Charlie's left, just over a hundred yards away, near the great hall. One of the mercenaries had managed to get into the center of the village, raising his rifle toward a group of small children huddled around a priest who had fallen on the front steps to the hall. The same priest who had met the party at the south entrance and decreed their lives forfeit.

Without a further thought, Deadeye ratcheted the lever on the carbine, raised the stock to his eye, took aim, and fired. The Russian dropped where he'd been standing, his rifle clattering to the gravel street. The *Goði* looked up, scanning the local area for the source of his relief, and saw Deadeye give him a one-handed salute. Rising with the children's assistance, the priest nodded back in respect.

Another burst of automatic gunfire rattled the afternoon air, as a mercenary rounded the outside northeast corner of the livery, mowing down an axe-wielding farmer, the blacksmith, and his stablemistress wife.

Deadeye ducked around the opposite corner enough to attract a quick burst from the Russian, clawing chunks of wood at his face. Deadeye recovered, and prepared to stand fire the next time he popped around. But the Russian suddenly fell to the road with a *thud*. Charlie slowly peeked around a second time and saw the fletched end of the arrow protruding from the top of the man's skull, the point jutting out beneath his chin. He'd collapsed face-forward, cheek to the ground, backside in the air. Deadeye glanced up toward the hayloft, and Sten saluted from the second-floor window.

The timber planking on the exterior walls of the stables erupted in an almost military cadence of impacts as the Russian machine gun blasted rounds across its side. Deadeye crouched near the bottom of the northwest corner, angling his head away. He cursed to himself and wracked his brain to figure out how to close the distance to the machine gun without a direct assault. He silently swore never to leave his Springfield sniper rifle when assigned to away duty. Never again.

Then he saw it: the Fedorov Avtomat lying near the main hall across the street. He'd yet to actually fire one of that model, but he assured himself the effective range simply had to be better than his lever-action carbine.

Sprinting across the road, Deadeye knew he'd be a target. Although his higher brain functions told him to run hunched over, he knew doing so would only slow him down. Instead, he went upright at full speed, as if running a hundred-yard dash.

The *Goði* and his flock of children had abandoned their vulnerable position in front of the great hall, so the street was largely empty of foot traffic. Charlie dived headfirst, as if stealing a base, tossing the Winchester to the ground as he rolled on his left shoulder and came up to a kneeling position, clearing the chamber of the Fedorov in a single graceful motion.

A quick duck-walk a meter to his left put him in the moderate cover of a large rain barrel adjacent to the entry of the hall. The rifle was heavier than the carbine, longer, with a thick wooden stock and a vertical hand grip in front of the curved magazine. It would have completely thrown him off if not for the fact that he was used to similar ergonomics on the Thompson submachine gun.

Casting a quick glance across his right shoulder, he saw the bright silver lozenge shape of the *Daedalus* descend over the footpath near the south end of the village. Despite the dwellings, reindeer corrals, and other structures between them, the airship was a large enough target that the machine gun crew would now be focusing most of their attention on it. Deadeye turned away from the *Daedalus*, scanning left along the meadow line and the grid of stone fences that divided the land. Several structures at the north end of town were now on fire, dark smoke and embers billowing out into the main street.

His heart sank. The bastards were torching houses.

Looking across the road to his right, he could now see the smithy and livery stable clearly, Sten perched in the hayloft of the massive building, keeping watch with an arrow nocked in the hunting bow. Deadeye waved him away from the window, urging him back to where Doc and Amaruq were securing Cipher into the sidecar of the Dugdalc. As Sten disappeared, Charlie turned his attention back across the meadow to where the machine gun crew were set up, only to find them missing.

A quick series of impacts along the road and up onto the rain barrel got his attention. The gun crew had moved their nest forward, and were now firing from behind a stone fence near the northeastern corner of town. That gave them superior cover and plenty of viable targets...including Deadeye.

The barrel was full, and had fortunately absorbed the rounds shot in his direction, although now it was leaking water from the holes perforating its front. Deadeye hefted the Fedorov and took aim, squeezing the trigger. Though braced for recoil, the kick was unexpected, and the three-round burst flew wildly high over the target. He adjusted his stance and fired again, and this time, chipped away at some of the rock in front of the gun crew. He felt his breath rise and fall in his chest. At least the weapon's range was comparable to theirs.

Charlie swallowed, thinking that what he could really use right now was four Lewis guns, like the ones in the front turret on the *Daedalus*.

☙

Buffeting winds subsided and the roiling storm system parted as the *Daedalus* shot out of the clouds over the mountain pass. Controls were instantly much more responsive.

Jack's eyes narrowed as he angled the steering yoke down over the lush alpine valley. He stopped working the stick of chewing gum, momentarily struck by its serene natural beauty and inherent unlikelihood. There was farmland, agriculture here. Herds of domestic caribou dashed to and fro in the grazing meadows. Rivers and creeks of pristine glacial water cut the valley into various sections, and a village of timber construction sat square in the center.

Tempted though he was to circle leisurely, taking in every tiny aspect of this place, he knew their current timetable did not allow for it, and the columns of smoke from the burning structures at the north end of the village drove the point home. Dozens of people in what looked like clothing from the Dark Ages scattered across the landscape. Some had bows, others were armed with spears. Still others clutched whatever farming tool they could. He couldn't see any kind of opposition, but he assumed they'd be further north in any case.

"Sparks," he hailed into the headset mic, "stand ready on the cargo door. This is probably going to be a quick stop."

Throttling down, Jack dropped altitude and came in low. The road that ran the center of the village was barely wide enough to accommodate the *Daedalus*, but if he could find a wider point—like that open square in front of some kind of great public hall. Yes, that would do nicely.

As the airship passed over the corrals and fields of crops, Jack noted what appeared to be the Dugdale, a passenger already bundled up in the sidecar. It stood just outside a dwelling of stone and timber, and it looked like Doc was astride the saddle.

Amaruq was there too, hitching the trailer sled to the rear of the motorcycle. A tall, bearded fellow who looked as if he'd wandered off a Cecil B. DeMille movie set crossed the road with an arrow in a bow of some kind. He seemed to be protecting the motorcycle and its occupants. All craned their necks upward as the great shark-like shadow loomed from above.

If that's Cipher in the sidecar, Jack thought, *she's probably injured. At least Doc and Amaruq are alive, and apparently well.* Jack swallowed and gritted his teeth as the *Daedalus* passed over. He wanted nothing more at that moment than to take Doc into his arms and never break the embrace.

Just as he began to wonder where the devil Charlie was in all of this, the sound of automatic gunfire brought his attention to the town square. There was a long-range exchange happening between Deadeye and what looked to be a machine gun crew set up behind a stone wall on the outskirts of the village.

Knowing full well that his airship would present a very large and inviting target, Jack angled in a left pivot around the nose, squeezing the trigger on the fire-linked Lewis guns in the nose turret. Four machine guns blasted away at the stone wall, spitting red tracers and hot lead. The Russian crew took cover, disappearing from sight.

Even if I don't eliminate them, Jack thought, *I can at least provide suppressive fire to cover our escape.*

A few random *pings* and *clangs* of bullets impacting the aluminum skeleton of the airship echoed through the bridge. There were clearly other enemy agents present, as well as the MG crew.

Jack keyed his *TALK* switch. "Okay, Sparks, get that cargo door down. I won't be able to help you back there. Gotta watch that machine gun and stay on the stick."

The *Daedalus* cargo door lowered down on whining hydraulic pistons. Sparks stood on the threshold, goggles on, an exotic weapon at the ready. Deadeye dashed to the yawning platform, clutching the Fedorov and the Winchester in either hand. He was glad to see

Sparks welcome him, and recognized the Tesla carbine that had been part of the standard AEGIS mission loadout since its introduction in 1925.

Quickly stashing the Winchester inside the cargo door, Deadeye adjusted the Fedorov and stepped back to cover the incoming crew.

Doc saw the *Daedalus* land just a couple of hundred yards away, watching for the cargo door to open. She opened the throttle of the Dugdale, but the packed gravel path kept it to an agonizing crawl. Amaruq sprinted ahead, gripping her spear, backpack slung across her shoulder. Sten kept pace, arrow still nocked in the bow.

Deadeye turned in a circle, surveying as much of the village as he could see. Gray smoke now cast a thick haze across the valley, orange embers drifting and falling with the breeze. The fighting had consolidated into small skirmishes spread throughout the vicinity. And while the Viking colony had greater numbers, there was no discounting the devastating effect of a well-trained mercenary with an automatic rifle.

A Russian agent popped up from the roof of a home across from the main hall, taking aim at the motorcycle as it crawled along the gravel road. Deadeye leveled the barrel of the Fedorov and squeezed off a quick burst, and the agent slumped to the roof.

Several more reports rang out, and Deadeye felt his left leg give way, sending him sprawling to the ground. Sparks stepped from the cargo ramp and aimed the Tesla gun toward where the shot had originated, sending a blast of blue-white lightning into—and through—the assailant.

Amaruq stopped to help Deadeye stand, grasping his waist as he hobbled toward the ship.

Doc angled the motorcycle toward the ramp, still some sixty yards distant. Gunshots erupted around the body of the cycle, kicking up dust and shards of rock. An agent crouched behind the water barrel at the great hall, taking Deadeye's former vantage.

A short burst of fire spit through the air, hitting the front fork of the Dugdale, wrenching the handlebars to the right, and Doc's arms with them. She cried out in surprise and frustration, but righted the steering immediately.

Sten noted the shot and drew his arrow back to his cheek. He let fly, and the long hunting arrow pierced the Russian's eye socket, erupting through the back of his skull.

Doc hunched over in the saddle and pushed the cycle forward. Forty yards.

Amaruq let go of Deadeye as he tumbled forward onto the cargo ramp. She caught a glimpse of the Winchester standing in the corner of the bay, just behind the door. "May I?" she asked. But before he could answer, the carbine was in her hands, and she was racking a cartridge into the chamber.

Thirty yards.

One agent broke around the back of a burning home to the north of the square. Amaruq turned to fire in time with Sten, who had another arrow at the ready. Bullet and shaft tore into the mercenary and he dropped to the ground. Another popped around the corner of a home across the path from the first.

Before Amaruq or Sten could ready another shot, a hail of arrows rained down from every direction, turning the man into a human pin cushion. Sten glanced up to see his hunters and their kin lining the roofs of the houses around the square. They had at least some cover from the north.

Twenty yards.

The converted snow-cycle whined forward, towing its sled over inconvenient terrain. Doc saw an agent peek over a stone fence to her right, and she shouted, pointing, "Over there!"

Sparks saw the man, and a blast of lightning from the Tesla gun made short, crispy work of him.

Ten yards.

The quad Lewis guns in the airship's nose opened up again at the stone wall across the meadow, tearing irregular castellations in the barrier. But the machine gun crew had relocated.

When the motorcycle finally hit the cargo ramp, Amaruq scrambled after it. Sparks took up a watch position on the ramp, surveying the starboard side of the airship with the Tesla gun at the ready.

As Sten turned to bid the crew farewell, the MG opened up into the square, tearing holes in the ground as the line of fire snaked along toward the aft section of the *Daedalus*. Sten collapsed, his right calf spattering blood on the ground.

Amaruq turned as he fell. He bellowed in pain and protest, and she flew from the cargo bay to grab hold of him.

Sparks turned to the half-wall where she'd immolated the last solo agent, and saw the machine gun crew back in action. Flipping the switch to full power, she pulled the trigger, arcing high voltage into their midst. The electric tendrils tapped and shifted, leaping from target to target, searing everything in their path.

Suddenly the lightning stopped, and the gun powered down with a declining hum. With the charge now depleted, Sparks ran to help

Amaruq, and together they hauled Sten up the cargo ramp into the ship.

Doc powered down the motorcycle's dynamo and went to the cargo door. As soon as Amaruq and Sparks were on board with Sten, she hit the industrial door control and the hydraulic arms began to pull up.

Pressing the *TALK* switch on the intercom next to the cargo door panel, Doc huffed through clenched teeth. "We're all aboard, Jack, get us the hell out of here!"

- CHAPTER 16 -

The *Daedalus* lumbered into the sky like an overfed goldfish, the controls sluggish from the recent addition of extra weight. Jack hauled back on the yoke and throttled to full speed, hoping for enough altitude to get them over the mountains surrounding the valley. Turbofans hummed as the airship drifted ever higher, knocked by competing winds as it flew.

"I need someone up on comms, PDQ," Jack announced into the headset.

Chaos was the reply. "Sorry, Captain," Sparks crackled back in his ears. "Give us a moment to sort out the wounded."

Worried, Jack gripped the flight yoke with both hands and continued to climb until the ship was out of range of ground fire. He suddenly missed the freedom and control of his old S.E.5 biplane. Currently the *Daedalus* felt more akin to flying a bloated whale with little to no visibility.

In the cargo bay, Sparks stepped through the assortment of crewmembers in various states of injury as Doc went to work stabilizing them in turn. Her medical bag was open alongside the portable aid kit from the wall, and bloody strips of bandage collected on the floor. Sparks had seen battlefields in her youth, in both the colonial warfare of the British, and the inter-tribal conflicts among the Kikuyu and their neighbors. Stowing the Tesla gun, she immediately went to Doc's aid, assisting in the bandaging of wounds and cleanup of blood-soaked cotton gauze.

Deadeye had a bullet wound in his left thigh, just above the knee, which not only left a clean exit but also managed to miss the femoral artery. Some iodine, a couple stitches on each side of his leg, and a tight dressing was all he needed.

Part of Sten's right calf had been torn away by multiple impacts, but again no bullet remained in the tissue. The wound was bloody, but not deadly. Doc cleaned and dressed his leg, then checked over the others. Amaruq had some scrapes and bruises, but no other injuries. Cipher remained unconscious and bundled up in the motorcycle sidecar.

Doc felt as if she'd been running at full speed since the encounter with the polar bears the previous night. But they weren't out of danger yet. She would have to summon the last of her reserves. "Sparks, Amaruq," she said softly, but with firm intent, "Please get Cipher to her bed and the boys squared away."

Deadeye and Sten managed to stand, leaning on one another. They had two good legs between them, and both were far too stoic to allow themselves to be nursed beyond a certain point. "We can handle ourselves," Charlie grunted. "You go up to the bridge and get on that radio detector. We must be getting awful close to the beacon."

Doc leaned in and planted a simple kiss on his cheek. "Thanks, Charlie," she said, heading to the door. Pausing, she turned and admonished the men once more. "Keep your weight off those limbs," she smiled. Then she was gone.

Jack heard the footsteps on the gantry and knew Doc was on the bridge without having to turn around.

"Honey, I'm home," she sighed, exhausted.

"How're we doing?"

"Couple clean bullet wounds, Cipher's recovering from surgery to repair damage from a bear attack."

"Bear attack?!"

Doc stepped down behind the pilot's chair and leaned over to kiss Jack on the crown of his head, gently squeezing his shoulders as she did. "Mmm. Bear attack. Polar bears. Two of them. Also a lost Viking colony, a deferred execution, and a probable Silver Star attack using Russian mercenaries." She stepped up to the radio console and slumped down in the chair, fastening the belt across her lap. "And I got to ride a reindeer."

Jack grinned. Unflappable. Dorothy Starr was simply unflappable. "So, pretty much your average Wednesday."

Doc laughed in a fit of full self-awareness, sliding the radio headset on. "Exactly," she chuckled.

Jack turned his attention forward through the windows. The sky was turning an inky black and icy water began to build up on the tempered glass. "Hold tight. It's gonna get rough until I get us through this system."

The ship bumped and jostled, swatted between competing currents. Lightning danced in the distance, splashing the clouds in strobing washes of purple and white.

"Not too likely to pick up anything in this," Doc muttered, fiddling with the tuner.

The ship bucked, caught in a sudden updraft, and Jack stiffened his legs to find better leverage with the steering yoke. He checked the power output on the engine console display: all running just under the red-line. He knew cutting throttle would only allow the ship to be kicked around within the maelstrom. Powering through the system, while not entirely a cakewalk, was the better option in the long run. If the engines continued their full output, anyway.

Another flash of lightning pierced the sky, the clap of thunder almost immediately on its heels. Rain and ice streamed across the bridge canopy windows. Jack didn't bother using the electric wipers—battling this level of precipitation was entirely futile. The bridge shook and shuddered again.

Then they were through.

The *Daedalus* soared out of the storm at twelve thousand feet, a crimson sun setting in the west. Flight controls suddenly became more responsive, and the change in ambient air pressure made Doc swallow to pop her ears.

"Well now," Jack muttered to himself. "Ain't that a nice little suit of armor?"

"What's that?" Doc asked from the comms console.

"Those storms," he replied. "They just hang over the mountains around the valley, make any aerial approach a dicey proposition."

"News flash, handsome. It's no better on the ground."

"*Touché.*"

Jack hit the *TALK* switch on his headset. "Captain to crew. We seem to have cleared the storm. I'm gonna throttle down and we'll take a moment to get our bearings. Carry on."

Powering the lateral thrust engines to ten percent Jack reckoned would keep the fans from freezing up. The giant outboard engines he set to one-quarter power. He angled back toward the coastline, putting the sun behind them.

"Now," he said, "where are we?" Flipping the release on the safety harness, Jack went to the navigation console and began rummaging through the cardboard tubes for the correct chart.

Ordinarily Doc would have taken proprietary offense at the invasion of her bridge station, but at the moment she had no energy to exert in such a fashion. In addition, she found herself getting sucked into the world of white noise and static as she scanned the airwaves for Silver Star radio chatter. The presence of snow-camouflaged Russian mercenaries in *Bålgard* had disturbed her more than she'd initially thought. It meant Aleister Crowley was using financial or political leverage to fill out his ranks, and didn't have to rely completely on his charismatic personality to put bodies in the field. Noting the time on the console clock, 19:57, she remembered something.

"We should be getting another broadcast from the beacon in about three minutes," she announced, checking her watch against the ship's time and finding herself a minute slow.

As she adjusted her timepiece, Jack nodded, staying focused on the chart of Greenland's northern coast.

Unrolling the laminated map onto the console desk, he produced a pocket compass at the same time. He set it on the flattened upper corner of the chart and noted that they were actually beyond the coastline, over frozen sea. "That valley...the mountains surrounding it..."

"It's an island," Doc finished. "About a mile offshore. We had to cross ice to get there."

"So unless the maps of the north Greenland coast are wrong, we're actually farther north and east than I thought."

"It's a good bet," Doc replied. "We know we're close. Now we just need to pinpoint the location of the signal."

"And retrieve the artifact, hopefully without engaging the Silver Star."

"A tall order," Doc sighed.

Jack laughed, marking an approximate location in waxed pencil on the chart. "That's all we pour at this bar," he said. Leaving the chart on the desk, he strode to the radio console, squeezing Doc's shoulders and kissing her on the top of the head, just as she had done to him earlier. "Anything?" he asked.

"No chatter currently," she answered. "They could be waiting for the signal, like us."

As the console clock ticked over to 20:00 hours, Jack could hear the low-pitched crackle of the electronic alien pulse. It repeated several times, then went silent. Immediately the nearby frequencies were a cacophony of radio messages—in voice and Morse code—and Doc knew they'd found the artifact's location.

"Sounds like they've found it," she said, her face ashen. But then she blinked, perking up as another message came through. "No, wait. They know where it's coming from. But their carrier can't fly out here, and their scout planes aren't outfitted for ice landings."

"Let's get a detector reading," Jack suggested.

Doc left the audio going in her headset as she turned to power on the radio detector. The familiar repeating pings erupted from the device as a bright green shape appeared on the circular monitor. It was oblong and enormous, and they both noted it was directly under the *Daedalus*. "Holy jeez!" she gasped.

"That's the *Osiris*," Jack explained. "Looks like it's not moving. Probably tied down in a canyon like the one we almost crashed in." He left the radio console and returned to the pilot's chair, strapping in and flipping the power toggles on the exterior running lights to the *Off* position. The radio detector historically had problems locating even large ships hidden beneath tree canopies or tall mountain ranges. This time, however, the granite peaks were spread far enough apart, and the *Daedalus* was almost directly overhead. Jack thought the *Osiris* would have had a tough time hiding from them in any conditions.

"What are you going to do?" Doc asked, suddenly very scared.

"I'm gonna find a nice, secluded, snowy canyon like the *Osiris*. We'll tie down for the night and keep tabs on the Silver Star via the radio. And you're gonna get some sleep, my dear."

The coastline lay obscured by a blanket of icy mist that undulated and shifted in place, forming a thick haze from sea level to five hundred feet. Jack lowered the *Daedalus* in a vertical descent, until the smaller airship was about a thousand feet over the *Osiris*. Still without radio detection equipment, the Silver Star would be unable to see them, and any radio anomaly would seem like a glitch or an echo. Pushing the throttle forward to thirty percent, he brought the airship's nose around and began searching the landscape for an equally hidden tie-down. He wanted to be inaccessible, yet close enough to engage if necessary, to save the artifact.

Jack found a shallow canyon of snow-covered granite along the coast, directly across the inlet from the *Osiris*, bringing the *Daedalus* down gently behind a screen of rock. There was land egress to the northeast, onto the frozen Arctic Sea. He landed nose-in, with the ring of rocky crags in front of them, so that the crew could access the ship via the cargo bay. Unfortunately, that eliminated the use of the ship's only armaments.

Sparks and Amaruq used the pneumatic piton guns to secure the airship from the outside, while Jack powered down the engines and went aft to check on his crew. He was surprised to see the addition of Sten, the impressive young Norseman in ancient garb who matched him in height and build. When it was explained how he and his hunting party had interceded on the away party's behalf, essentially saving Cipher's life, Jack welcomed him aboard with much gratitude. He offered Sten his stateroom for the duration of his visit, and promised they'd drop him back home when all of this was over. The Norseman was gracious, but declined the offer of a return trip as he locked eyes with a certain Inuit guide who blushed red.

They set up a four-hour watch. Sparks and Amaruq stood first, while the injured crewmembers rested. Jack and Doc took the opportunity to reconnect in private, making love in Doc's quarters, after which he left her alone to slumber.

As Jack ambled through the main saloon, coffee mug in hand, he peered out through the gondola windows, finding nothing but a light gray sheen of collected snow. Three of his crew were injured. Every one of them was exhausted. The odds weren't terrific, but then they rarely were. And yet, they were so close to the objective. He took a seat near one of the icy windows and leaned back, contemplating various strategies for whatever came their way tomorrow.

He rested the mug on his belly, which rose and fell with his breathing. In a few moments, he had drifted off into a fitful sleep.

- CHAPTER 17 -

Jack arose from his truncated rest with a kink in his neck, but otherwise refreshed and ready to depart for the source of the signal. The crew who were mobile began to assemble in the main saloon. Coffee was brewed, and a rudimentary breakfast of oat-bars and hard-boiled eggs consumed. Radio checks at 00:00 hours and 04:00 hours had yielded identical signal broadcasts to the prior events. The source of the signal was determined—or really "guesstimated"—to be about four miles from their current location, and three miles of that distance off the northern coast, in the frozen Arctic Sea.

Jack realized as he did a head count that he, Doc, Amaruq, and Sparks were the only uninjured members of the crew, and he made an executive decision.

"Doc and I are going to take the cycle. Everyone else stay back here, monitor the radio and be ready to take off at a moment's notice. We'll try to be quick."

Deadeye's demeanor dropped and he instantly became livid. "No way, no how, Cap. I might be limpin' a little, but I ain't just waitin'—"

"It's not a request, Charlie." Jack cupped a hand over his shoulder and fixed him with a brotherly look. "Save your strength. Depending on Cipher's recovery, you might need to fly the ship out of here." He turned to Sten and Amaruq, standing together by the galley counter, sipping hot coffee. Sten was visibly taken with the beverage, after the initial bitterness. "I want to thank you two," Jack said. "Amaruq, you have been an expert guide. And Sten, several of my crew owe you their lives. If we get out of this in one piece, we'll take you anywhere you want to go."

The tall Viking shook his hand, but said nothing. Amaruq sensed he, too, wasn't wild about being held back from action. He'd also made it clear he had no intention of returning to his secluded green island at the top of the world.

Jack raised an eyebrow at Doc. "How is Cipher, by the way?"

"Stable," Doc replied, sipping from the metal mug. "Sleeping. She needs lots of rest."

"Of course," said Jack. "Let her sleep." Rinsing his mug in the galley sink and hanging it on the wall hook, he turned and found Sparks eying him from the starboard dining table. "What's the ship's status?"

"All systems normal," she answered. "Running the heaters to the turbofans nonstop. We can fly at any time."

"Outstanding." Jack glanced around the small room, meeting each face and pair of eyes with a solemn smile. "So here's the thing. Some of you have been with us for years, and some considerably less so. But I value every soul on board this ship, and that's why I need you to stay behind. If anything happens to Doc or myself, someone is going to need to get the *Daedalus* back, and tell AEGIS what happened here. They've got to know, and they've got to prepare. Because if Crowley gets his hands on an alien artifact that can resurrect the dead, then the world becomes a lot scarier and more dangerous in the blink of an eye. Now we're gonna try to stop that from happening, if we can. But if not..."

There was silence in the cabin as Jack's gaze roamed from person to person, all eyes swollen with impending tears. "Alright," he said finally. "Let's get to work."

Jack and Doc donned their snow gear. Ammo was checked and re-stocked for the journey. Jack grabbed one of two Thompson guns from the armory, slapped in a single drum and slung it over his shoulder. Each of them also snapped up a pair of fragmentation grenades and a Tesla grenade, hooking the small mark-2 "pineapples" to points on a personal web harness, or in Jack's case, his gun belt. The Teslas were stashed with the backup ammunition in a canvas shoulder bag, strapped atop of the sole remaining field radio on the rear rack of the motorcycle. He hoped they wouldn't need to call for backup, seeing what sorry shape their backup was actually in.

Doc unpacked her field notes from her canvas satchel and handed the pile of notebooks and papers to Deadeye. "If anything happens, here's my research on the artifact. Make sure it gets back to AEGIS Command."

Deadeye nodded compliance, knowing full well that she would hand over those notes herself, if he had anything to say about it.

Then they were off, the Dugdale's dynamo whirring as the vehicle departed the aft cargo bay. Jack rode in the saddle, Doc in the sidecar, scanning ahead with her field binoculars. The hydraulic legs of the cargo door whined as it closed, Amaruq, Sten, and Deadeye all exchanging glances as they watched the snow cycle disappear into the mist.

"There's no visibility out here," Doc said.

Jack wiped the beading water from his goggles with a gloved hand and chuckled. "You don't say?"

About a hundred yards beyond the canyon, the uneven snow began a gradual decline, finally leveling off to a flat plane of frosty white over dark gray, and the mist seemed to grow thin. As they drove forward onto the flat expanse, Jack realized they'd left the solid ground of the coast and were now riding on Arctic ice.

As they finally left the gauzy bank of fog in their wake, Jack took note of the rudimentary horizon: a faint line separating the pale gray morning sky from the blue-white icy floor below. The dynamo buzzed like a housefly as they motored for miles over the flat, snowy wilderness—their own party a pale gray dot in a vast white landscape.

Eventually, the precipitation lifted. With visibility much improved, Jack squinted into the distance. Perhaps four hundred yards ahead, a massive shape broke the horizon line.

Doc squirmed in the sidecar, binoculars pressed to her eyes, mouth agape. "Jack, do you see that? Dead ahead..."

"I see *something*," he replied. "Not sure what."

"It...it looks like a wooden ship," Doc marveled, checking her own vision and then returning to the field glasses. "Locked in the ice. Masts are sheared away. Amazed it hasn't sunk at some point in the last eighty years."

"You think that's the *Lougen?*" Jack posed, immediately hearing how silly the question sounded.

Doc pursed her lips, keeping her eyes to the binoculars. "You know of any other missing ships at this location?"

Jack cracked a weathered smile, but his focus was on the approach to the icebound ship. There was no kind of cover anywhere, no place to hide if fired upon. They'd simply have to hope nobody had beaten them to the vessel, or if they had, that their approach wouldn't be detected. As he wrestled with their strategically boxed-in predicament, the sound of a tree limb snapping from its trunk vibrated up from below, and suddenly Jack's attention was forced to the ice beneath the Dugdale's treads. Already he could see cracks running like a spiderweb deep within the ice. He knew the frozen surface was thick enough to hold them for the time being, but couldn't guarantee how long. So much of this mission continued to be a guessing game, and Jack was quickly running out of guesses.

"What's that sound?" Doc asked, peering over the side of the car.

"Just the deep ice cracking," Jack explained, chillingly nonchalant. "Shouldn't actually break up any time soon. But just the same..."

"Give it some gas, Jeeves," she nodded, gesturing forward.

The snow cycle's dynamo whined on as Jack opened the accelerator and closed with the dark shape in the ice.

CR

No sooner had the cargo door clamped shut than Deadeye, Amaruq, and Sten began suiting up for an unauthorized shore excursion. Layers of clothing went on, weapons and supplies were gathered, and nary a word was spoken. At least until Sparks discovered the trio coming aft again.

She raised an eyebrow at Charlie, who halted in the engine room door.

"Don't try to stop us," he warned, somewhat unconvincingly.

The Kenyan mechanic folded her arms and chuckled. "No one's stopping you, Deadeye. Go on through." Deadeye stepped into the engine room and flagged the other two toward the cargo bay. As they passed through, she added, "All I ask is that you don't get yourself killed."

Deadeye clamped his wide hands on her shoulders and winked. "That's the idea," he quipped. "Too many awkward conversations... and all the *paperwork!*" They embraced quickly, and he was gone.

As they entered the cargo area, it became clear they would not have the benefit of motorized transportation.

"With Cap and Doc on the Dugdale, looks like we'll be hoofin' it," Deadeye muttered.

Amaruq wasn't sure, but it sounded almost like a complaint. It couldn't be as simple as that. Her eyes caught the glint of a twelve-foot aluminum strut lying next to the tow-sled. A roll of shade canvas lay adjacent to it in the corner. As she looked over the contents of the bay, a thought occurred to her, and as she turned to mention it to Sten, she saw he'd clearly had the same idea. "If we take that shade canvas," she began, "and lash it to that strut..."

Sten smiled. "And we tie it to the sledge, then we have transport."

Deadeye was intrigued, but cautious. "What, you mean we're gonna *sail?*"

"Indeed!" Sten nodded, without a hint of irony.

Amaruq shook her head. "Not the whole way. We'll have to push through the snow on foot. But once we're on the ice, we can ride."

"Well," Deadeye sighed, "we're not sailing ice sleds if everyone's standing around. Let's hop to it."

It took under five minutes to patch together the rudimentary mast and sail, securing it to the nose of the sled at a severe backward angle with something Deadeye found to be the true new wonder of the modern age: nylon cord. Sparks even made an appearance to inspect their handiwork, and make a few suggestions.

With the vehicle made ready, Deadeye packed it with both his Springfield rifle and his trusty Winchester repeater, snapping his Spanish cavalry pistol into the canvas holster on his hip. A small field pack containing water, rations and sundry tools followed.

The cargo door hummed downward on hydraulic legs, becoming a ramp to the frozen world outside.

The trio was then gone, and Sparks hit the button once more to shut out the cold.

- CHAPTER 18 -

Jack slowed the motorcycle to a crawl as they approached the giant wooden vessel from the stern. Though encased in multiple layers of ice and frost, her nameplate was generally legible: it was indeed the *Lougen*. As they had perceived from a distance, her masts had weakened and snapped by Arctic winds long ago. She sat low in the ice, undisturbed by the occasional subterranean torque and snap of shifting, buckling floes feet below the surface.

Doc noted the ship was facing southeast. Probably heading home to Norway via the Greenland Sea, before whatever had happened to strand her here.

Jack switched off the Dugdale and signaled to Doc for their approach. They quietly disembarked, each pushing their goggles up to get a clearer view.

The area around the ship was oddly still, and devoid of any other people, at least from their vantage at the stern. Doc gestured to Jack that she was going up onto the deck, and he gave her a boost to the rail, which she rolled across, disappearing from view.

Jack plucked one of the Colts from its canvas housing and began to circle the massive merchant vessel on the ground. Stepping softly on the snow-dusted frozen ground, he crept toward the bow on the starboard, south-facing side. The hull was in surprisingly good condition for having been locked in the ice for almost a century. Covered in a twinkling sheen of crystals, she looked to have been a sound example of 19th century Nordic maritime construction.

As he rounded the prow, Jack noted the bowsprit had been snapped off halfway down, similar to the way in which the masts had departed. A mountain of ice and packed snow had built up around the bow, creating a slick hill, upon which his boots could not possibly find purchase. His eyes roamed the frost-covered surface of the wooden ship, but a boxy shape broke her elegant line, and Jack realized there was a vehicle parked off the port bow, on the ice.

Stepping closer, he saw the factory black finish and bucket chassis, recognizing it as a Ford Model T open-bed truck, converted to arctic operations. Two wheels on each side at the rear of the vehicle rotated a belt tread in much the same way as a tank or tractor. The front axle had been replaced with a completely different spring system resting on a pair of thick skis. Jack sneaked toward the cab and peered into the window. The vehicle was empty, but there was another parked just a few yards away to the east.

He did some quick math in his head. The Silver Star wouldn't take multiple vehicles carrying one man apiece. If each snow crawler seated two, then they could anticipate no fewer than four field agents on site. And that didn't include any grunts who may have been transported in the truck beds. Then again, he knew they were competing with the *Osiris*, and although Jack had never met the supercarrier's commander, he presumed that, like most Silver Star officers, he had a penchant for power. If they were lucky, this team of agents would be small. Hand-picked and almost certainly elite, but small.

Just as he was wondering why they hadn't left a sentry to watch the vehicles, Jack heard the distinct sound of water trickling onto a surface and splattering to the ground. The cloud of steam rising told him there indeed was a sentry, and he was taking a restroom break behind the second vehicle.

Scurrying between the cab of the trailing Ford and the bed of the lead truck, Jack holstered his Colt and undid the safety strap on his field knife, unsheathing it with one deft motion. The Silver Star commando was in light gray cold weather fatigues, parka hood down, displaying the back of a white knit cap. Steam continued to rise as the man whistled an old German folk tune. Jack took six graceful, silent steps, and in a single balletic move, encircled the agent's neck and opened his throat. As the man collapsed, blood painting the ice a dark crimson, Jack pulled the MP-18 from his victim's shoulder and removed the magazine, tossing it away onto the ice. He threw the weapon in the opposite direction, watching as it skittered and spun. As the familiar acidic odor met his nose and the smoke began to rise in black tendrils, Jack left the man's body where it fell, rushing to the side of the ship to leap aboard—and hopefully find Doc.

CR

Doc rolled onto the aft deck and came up in a crouch with barely a sound. The lodestone hung around her neck on its silver chain, glowing a soft blue and humming with a stirred mystical energy. The planking on the ship's decks looked sturdy, although slick with ice and frost. As she'd seen from below, the masts had broken off some time in the distant past. The canvas sails that once draped the decks as tent shelters from the elements lay in frozen shreds on the deck, frost glistening like a diamond carpet. Various barrels and crates lay stationed across the main, fore, and aft decks, unopened and undisturbed. No sign of recent habitation met her eyes, no tracks in the white dust that she could see. She unsnapped the holster on her left hip, cross-drawing the .38 police revolver from within.

The lodestone pulsed white, its harmonics ringing.

Doc felt suddenly nauseous. A low-pitched thrum began beneath the deck, built quickly, and shot outward in a sort of shockwave that knocked her off her feet. It was the same cadence and tone she and Cipher had been studying. It was the alien signal.

Doc leaned up on her elbow, pushed the opening of her glove aside and checked her watch: 5:48 a.m. The signal wasn't due until 0800. Something had changed. Gathering herself to a standing position, she took a deep breath and blinked her eyes in the stinging cold.

She sidestepped past the giant ship's wheel, looking past the display of icicles pointing downward from every surface. Her gaze was on main deck, just behind the foc'sle. When she finally got an unobstructed view, the blood drained from her cheeks and she gasped.

The man stood, tall and regal in his Silver Star officer's uniform, white parka, and gleaming black boots, eyes fixed on the object he held in his hand: an orb about the size of a croquet ball, with a dark metallic sheen, inscribed in strange glyphs only a select few on this planet had ever seen, much less understood. The sphere had opened at its midsection revealing a cylinder at its center, alien shapes glowing emerald green, pulsing in a slow rhythmic dance.

Almost as if it were breathing.

Oh no, Doc thought, her mind swimming. *Oh no, no, no.*

There was a flurry of motion to her left, and Jack vaulted the port rail onto the aft deck. She was glad to see him, if only because this could mean their last time on Earth together.

His arrival caught the attention of the officer holding the artifact. "Oh, hallo!" he hailed in Dutch-tinged English, his cordial tone disconcerting. "You are from AEGIS, yes?"

Doc shuddered. "He's got the artifact," she warned under her breath to Jack.

"Captain Jack McGraw, of the airship *Daedalus*." He caught himself saluting, then thought better of it. "I assume I'm addressing the commander of the *Osiris*?"

The officer regarded them through discerning gray eyes. His thin line of a mouth drew up in the approximation of a smile. "Captain Ernst Hummel, at your service." Clicking his boot heels together formally, he bowed slightly at the waist.

Jack unshouldered the Tommy gun and took up a stance at the aft deck railing in front of the helm. "My, my, my," he marveled, full of bravado. "Not the *Schwarzhund*? The Black Dog of the Eastern Front? Your reputation precedes you." He wasn't lying. Jack knew of the Black Dog's exploits in the Baltic and Eastern Front during the Great War. He was not a man to be underestimated.

"Indeed," Hummel replied with a reptilian grin. "As has yours, *Captain Stratosphere*."

Jack rolled with the man's sarcastic use of his nickname, determined not to let him see weakness. "After your doings on the Black Sea during the war, I gotta admit I was surprised to find you working with Russian soldiers out here."

"They were mercenaries. They were well paid. And most of them are now dead, thanks to you and the people of that valley."

Jack chose to revel in the somewhat backhanded compliment, but let the moment pass quickly. "Yeah. Sorry about that. So, whatcha got there, Chief?"

"Oh," Hummel sighed, "just a powerful alien artifact, imprisoned in the hold of this vessel for eighty years."

"An artifact you know nothing about!" Doc piped up from the top of the aft deck ladder. She glanced at Jack, who threw her an exasperated look. He didn't often chide her; in the context of their relationship she was truly an equal and free to express herself. Not that he could have stopped her if he wanted to. But now she saw that Jack had been trying to keep the focus on him—and off her—probably so that when he made a move against Hummel, she could swoop in and retrieve the orb.

Hummel squinted across the length of the ship. "Doctor Dorothy Starr, I presume? You also have quite the reputation as an occult scholar within my organization."

Jack tried to get Hummel's attention back on him. "That's right. Your organization. Say, I thought Maria Blutig was Crowley's second banana. Why isn't she heading up this little shindig?"

Disinterested in the further conversation, Hummel returned his gaze to the rotating kaleidoscope of illuminated glyphs within the center of the orb. The pulsing colors and shapes were hypnotic. "Maria Blutig is...currently indisposed."

Jack cocked his head, intrigued. "Well *that's* interesting news." Aiming the Thompson at Hummel, he stuck out his broad jaw. "Tell you what, Chief. You hand over the artifact, and we can chat more about current events at our leisure."

Without looking up, Hummel waved his left hand, and six commandos appeared in the doorways from below deck, three on either side of the ship. Each was dressed in gray Arctic fatigues and a white parka. Six bolts on six MP-18s ratcheted back.

Just like that, Jack and Doc were outnumbered and outgunned.

"No," Hummel mused in a sing-song timbre, "I don't think I will be handing over the artifact. Nor will there be any further discussion." He nodded a head of jet black hair toward the afterdeck. "Shoot them."

- CHAPTER 19 -

Marissa Singh's eyes fluttered open and darted around the cold gray laminate walls of her shipboard quarters. She recognized the interior, and could feel she was in her bunk. Grunting with effort, she tried to sit upright, but was easily stopped by the firm hand of Dhakiya Kitur. The young mechanic smiled and eased her back down to her pillow.

"What...what happened?" Cipher croaked, her throat dry from the chill air. "I-I remember...polar bears?"

Sparks nodded, offering Cipher a sip of water from a tin cup. "You were attacked," she said, relating the adventure of the past day and a half. "Doc fixed you up, but you've been out for a long time. Missed some things."

"Where is everyone?" Cipher inquired, swallowing half the contents of the cup in a single audible gulp.

"Jack and Doc went to go get the artifact," Sparks explained. "And the others went to back them up."

Cipher began to stir, not so much her strength returning as simply not wanting to be asleep anymore. "We need to get ready," she said, and as she pushed up on her arms, a jolt of agony stabbed through her shoulder and took her breath away. As she fell back against the pillow, Sparks smiled knowingly.

"I understand," she said. "But take it slow. I was just heading onto the bridge to monitor the radio. Let's get a cup of coffee, and we'll go together."

Cipher nodded in silent compliance. Within moments, she was standing upright and Sparks had her braced for transit.

"Don't worry," Dhakiya assured her. "You'll get your land legs back in time."

They stopped in the galley, and Cipher leaned against the counter as Sparks poured a couple of mugs of hot coffee. She passed one to the injured comms officer, and they clinked the mugs together in a toast.

"Cheers," said Cipher. "Thanks for checking in on me."

Sparks winked, sipping from her cup.

Then the muted drumbeat of distant gunfire echoed in bursts from across the frozen terrain outside, and the two scrambled immediately to the bridge.

○⊃

The aluminum sled rocketed across the ice, close-hauled to take advantage of the strong northerly wind. Deadeye sat forward, near the rudimentary mast, scanning the horizon ahead. He could already see the massive black shape of the wooden ship locked in the ice. He glanced back at Amaruq and gestured at the object. The young guide nodded and shifted the sail, adjusting their trajectory as she did so.

Sten rode the rear of the sled, like a musher with the wind at his command instead of a dog team. He had taken a liking to these strangers from the world outside, and was looking forward to experiencing that world. But first, he would help them retrieve this object which had awakened the dead. Hel would not be happy that such a device existed, and was stealing souls from her domain.

The sound of gunfire carried across the ice. Deadeye knew they hadn't a moment to lose.

"Get down!" Jack bellowed, more out of habit than actual utility, as a blaze of automatic gunfire trailed across the deck planks and frozen hardware.

Doc was already down, dragging herself prone to a hiding spot behind a stack of old supply crates on the aft deck. "Good advice," she quipped. "What now?"

Jack popped up from behind a thick water barrel, looking for all the world like a giant prairie dog. The Thompson barked a short burst, and one of the commandos dropped in place, black smoke rising from the body before it hit the deck. "Fire back when you can," he instructed. "And try not to get shot."

Doc rolled her eyes. Glancing down at her left arm, she felt the weight of the ancient Greek vambrace under the down parka, mumbling the ancient incantation to activate its power. *Should have led with that,* she thought. *Still, better late protective magic than no protective magic.* Leaning to one side, she could get a scant view of the forward section, and saw that Captain Hummel was climbing the steps to the forecastle, still staring in rapt attention at his glowing prize. *Look at him,* she thought. *He has no idea how to work the artifact, or what it does if he could work it.*

She fired a single shot, which went wide, gouging into a crate opposite the base of the main mast.

Jack opened up a second time, the Tommy gun spitting fire and lead. A second and third commando fell, and immediately began to dissolve. That took care of the three on the port side. As he shuffled from his meager cover, he caught a brief glimpse of the other three soldiers, clumped together in the corner adjacent to the stepladder to the fore deck. One had his weapon gripped in a single hand, using the other to hold the icy handrail as he tried to climb the steps to join Hummel. A single shot rang out, and the man fell to the deck below, sizzling and smoldering.

Jack turned to look at Doc, who returned his glance with a competent wink, gun smoke wafting from the barrel of her .38.

"We can't let him leave with the orb, Jack!" Doc warned.

"I know," Jack huffed. "I'm trying to think of how to get to him."

"Frag grenade?"

"I don't want to damage the artifact."

"Good thinking. What about a Tesla grenade?" Doc suggested. "Stun them?"

Jack shook his head. "Left them on the bike...with the radio."

Doc rolled her eyes again, so hard it hurt. "I can't take you anywhere."

Another blaze of suppressive fire clawed through the afterdeck, spitting icy splinters into the misty morning air.

"And I can't take Tesla grenades anywhere, apparently."

No sooner had the word *grenades* exited his mouth than a small metal object clattered over the side to the main deck, sending fingers of electricity arcing through the commandos. The two men danced spasmodically in place for a moment, then collapsed in a heap. Smoke began to waft from the unconscious bodies immediately.

Deadeye slipped over the deck rail, Winchester in hand, followed by Sten and Amaruq. The tracker clutched Deadeye's Springfield rifle. The Viking brandished his hunting spear.

The dark-haired marksman threw a look back at his captain. "I found it in your saddlebag. Hope you don't mind."

Jack's heart swelled with a broad range of conflicting emotions, but Hummel looked like he was trying to make an exit. There was no time for pleasantries, nor for a military chewing-out. "Deadeye! Get Hummel—get the artifact!"

Jack rushed past the ship's wheel to the steps, and Doc followed. As he leaped down the ladder from the aft deck, the sound of snapping timber shook through the legs of everyone aboard. The deck shuddered as in a massive earthquake. The frozen sea around them was breaking into separate fragments, which were crushing the ship.

But the unearthly growls that followed weren't of the wood-cracking variety. The doors on either side of the forecastle leading below to the crew quarters suddenly burst into flying shards of debris, and a snarling horde of angry corpses scrabbled up to the deck, eyes afire with emerald green light.

Having dealt with the native *draug* only days ago, Jack knew this would not be a clean or noble fight. The war had taught him that few fights were either of those things. But fight they would have to, for their very lives. Jack's intent was to overwhelm the ravening ghouls as quickly as possible, at least buying Deadeye the necessary time to get away from the group and take Hummel down.

Before he could shout a single command, the ghouls were on them. They swarmed across the decks, frozen 19th century naval clothes snapping and rupturing with their movement. Jack's Tommy gun raged at the mass of rampaging corpses, rending chunks of petrified skull and bone into the morning air until at last the drum was empty. Two creatures fell, but the overall effort appeared futile.

The mob pressed forward, slashing at them with savage talon hands. There were perhaps a dozen, though in their state it seemed like twice that number. But because it was not in Jack's nature to surrender without significant resistance, he had shucked both pistols before the Thompson gun clattered to the floor. The twin Colts thundered, sending pieces of the ghouls across the decks and out over the ice.

As Jack emptied both clips into the ravening mob, Doc reasoned these were probably the corpses of sailors who had died on the ship, leaving a ready cohort of soldiers for Hummel some eighty years later. This cemented her theory that the device was broadcasting a wave of mystical power that reanimated the dead. Dead *people*, anyway. And Hummel was figuring out its control mechanism, like a child with a *Mah Jongg* set, but no rulebook. For some reason, however, the *Osiris* captain hadn't made a move to escape, only watch the carnage from a higher vantage point, under better cover. Although the radio signal appeared to reanimate dead humans at significant range, perhaps actually controlling them required proximity.

Sten bounded to the head of the group, holding his spear horizontally across his body like some sort of barricade. The ghouls pressed against him, skeletal hands clawing, bare teeth snapping. Doc fired into the ghoulish mass and began to work her way to the rail, figuring that if Hummel tried to flee, she could run for the snow cycle and chase down whatever transportation he possessed. Her cylinder was empty before she knew it, and it had done little to no good. She looked toward Deadeye, who had made it up the ladder to the foredeck and was trading shots with Hummel, who crouched behind a crate with the orb in one hand, a Luger in the other.

Amaruq ducked a slashing arm and fired the Springfield from her hip. The shot was deafening, the bullet blowing a hole through the ghoul and flinging a frozen vertebra out the other side. She fumbled with the bolt, glancing to her right just as one of the writhing horde punched into Sten's abdomen and pulled forth a handful of internal organs.

The Viking bellowed in anger and agony, though stoically stood his ground, holding back the mob with his hunting spear. Amaruq screamed in horror at the sight of Sten's innards spilling onto the deck, mirroring her cousin's state just forty-eight hours previous.

"Go!" Sten cried, legs beginning to tremble. The *draug* were pushing forward, arms reaching, grabbing. The furs on his arms and chest were savagely slashed and torn.

Amaruq screamed again, this time in abject defiance. Slapping the bolt back into place, she raised the rifle again, firing just as the ghoul with the hole in its torso knocked the barrel away—putting Sten in the line of fire. This time the thunderclap signaled the quick end to a grisly ordeal. The bullet entered under his jaw and exited his right temple, his lifeless body crumpling to the frozen deck.

A singular numbness entered her almost instantly, seeping into every corner of her body as her mind tried to process what had just happened. The ghoul attacked immediately, clawing and rending with its frozen bones. As she collapsed under the weight of the animated corpse, the rifle pinned under her arms, despair began to consume her. A bony finger sliced at her face, opening wounds on her cheekbone and precariously close to her eye. She felt the pressure of Doc's arm as it flung across her chest, Amaruq's vision exploding in dull flashes of aquamarine at every swipe of the ghoul's bony hand. Somehow, some molecule of will remained alive within her, and in a series of small hand movements, she pulled the rifle bolt back, ejecting the spent shell, and pushed it forward again. Her left hand wrestled the barrel under the ghoul's head, with its patches of icicle-dripping beard on an almost mummified skeletal face. If she got out of this alive, she knew that face would haunt her dreams forever. The shot rang out and Amaruq's left ear went deaf—all she could hear was a high-pitched ringing. But the ghoul's head had been caved out through the back, the twitching body rolling and writhing on the deck.

Hummel took note of the accident below on the main deck, musing to himself. "Most interesting," he mumbled, twisting the top half of the orb. Another pulse of mystical energy erupted from the artifact, washing outward with the force of a sonic boom.

On the main deck, the party stumbled collectively, knocked to their knees by the almost invisible shockwave. Doc knew instantly what Hummel had done.

The three staggered back to their feet—along with Sten.

His eyes opened slowly, glowing with green fire.

- CHAPTER 20 -

Jack had had enough.

"Grenade!" he warned, pulling the pin on the fist-sized, pineapple-shaped explosive and rolling it across the icy deck planks. It skittered between the legs of the *draug*, where it banked off the side of a crate and toppled through the doorway, down the stairs to the deck below. The explosion sent shards of wood and rusted metal, along with its own shrapnel, rocketing out of the doorway. While the party managed to duck away in time, the explosion successfully mowed down a couple of ghouls, and ignited whatever material was still flammable in the crew quarters. Lamps of kerosene or whale oil, frost-covered charts, books—anything that could catch fire, did.

"Ship's on fire!" came Jack's update over the crackle of the spreading conflagration below decks, and the shuffling of reanimated corpses.

Hummel watched the events unfold below and cast a glance over the bow toward the mountainous coastline. There, on the horizon, were four more snow crawlers, each carrying four Silver Star reinforcements. If he made a run for it now, he might be able to get to his own snow car and get to safety while the AEGIS field team was still preoccupied with the fire and the dead he'd awakened.

Deadeye watched from his cubby behind the crates, snapping cartridge after cartridge into the Winchester until the internal magazine was full.

As smoke began to billow from the deck hatches and doorways, the *draug* maintained their assault. Now each of the three on the main deck were faced with three of their own ghouls, all glowing green eyes and frozen bones.

And Sten.

Recalling how little relative damage firearms had done in their first encounter with the *draug* hunters their first day, Jack opted for more direct measures. As both pistols were empty anyway, he flipped them over, clutching the barrels in each hand, using the grips as bludgeons. He waded into the thick of the creatures, striking and pounding with two small nickel-plated maces, sending jawbones flying and shattering rib cages.

With the immediate pressure literally lifted off them, Doc helped Amaruq upright. Together they stood, letting anger and adrenaline take hold.

Doc located a three-foot piece of door frame torn loose by the grenade. Holstering her revolver, she grabbed the plank by its base and swung for the bleachers, taking one *draug*'s head clean away. Amaruq gripped the Springfield much as Sten had done with his spear, slamming ghouls with the heavy walnut stock. It had come to the messy, brutal fighting they'd all known was coming.

Sten stood at the center of the mob and stared at her, emerald eyes burning.

As she punched and clubbed her way into the fray, she told herself it wasn't really him, that he was lost to her, lost to them all. It was merely his sundered body, nothing left that was uniquely Sten. Tears streamed from her burning eyes as she swung the rifle stock as a club, bashing frozen bones indiscriminately.

If Sten was in the way of her rampage, she didn't notice where one enemy ended and another began, nor did the reanimated man make any move to stop her.

By the time she'd worked her way through the mob to the other side, Sten lay beneath a pile of dismembered corpses, and Amaruq made no attempt to investigate further.

Suddenly Hummel burst from behind the crate and leaped over the deck rail to the slope of ice beneath the bow of the ship.

Deadeye was after him instantly, skating down the hill on the soles of his boots, firing the repeater toward Hummel's legs. His shots went wide enough to miss flesh, but burrowed into the ice at the bottom of the slope. Surface fissures began to extend from the impacts, and Deadeye saw the first lateral fracture appear just as Hummel reached the terminus.

The Black Dog found the flat plane of the ice and jinked to the left, toward the parked snow cars only yards away. Deadeye was hot on his six, dodging aside as Hummel snapped off two blind shots from the Luger.

Suddenly Hummel was at the first vehicle, and had to make a decision. Two hands, one needed by the artifact. He tossed the pistol away and grabbed the door handle to access the cab of the snow crawler.

Deadeye opened fire with the repeater, shredding Hummel's knees into hamburger. The *Schwarzhund* cried out as his weight dropped beside the vehicle, the cuff of his parka snagging on the door handle. He felt deep ruptures radiating outward from the ship, ultimately finding the surface ice, exploding like pressurized glass beneath the truck and all around them.

There was a bone-shattering *crack*, then a second, as the ground beneath Hummel's bloody legs sundered and split apart, and the snow crawler plunged into the icy water, taking the *Osiris* captain with it, door handle still hooked through his sleeve.

Contact with the near-freezing water sent a shock throughout his body, and Hummel gasped for breath that never came. He watched the glowing green sigils on the orb shift and rotate, a beautiful display as he was dragged down into cold darkness. For a moment, he thought he felt pressure on his wrist, but he could no longer feel the device, or much of anything.

He was aware of the sensation of releasing the orb, which continued to glow as a strange hand took hold of it and kicked upward, toward the surface.

༄

The moment he heard the first deep crack of ice, Deadeye sprinted, tossing his rifle aside. He flew into the icy water head first, grabbing at Hummel's wrist to make him let go of the device. His fingers finally parted, and as the Ford dragged him into the depths, Deadeye saw a brief look of surprise on his face before he was lost in the dark.

Charlie kicked for the surface, for air. The cold had an instant effect on his body, sapping the heat and strength from his muscles. His right hand shot into the air just above the water, clutching the orb.

Immediately hands were on him, grabbing him, pulling him from the sea onto the solid flat ice. He rolled to his back, coughing up salt water and wheezing in agony. "C-c-cold..." was all he could manage, lips blue, pale cheeks flushed with scarlet freckles from his burst capillaries.

The collapsing surface ice had taken the second snow crawler as well as the first, and had torn loose from the ship, which was now visibly aflame and beginning to shear away from the ice on the other side.

Amaruq shed her parka and put it over Deadeye to help warm him, and Jack did the same. He rubbed his comrade's arms to generate more heat.

Deadeye lifted his right arm, shivering, to offer up the artifact. "H-h-here you g-go, Doc..."

Eyes wide in trepidation, Doc took the metal sphere from him, gazing over its surface at the illuminated alien symbols. She'd been studying the written Martian language long enough to recognize most of the individual characters, and to have some theories about what a symbol meant. Pressing her thumb over one of the symbols, she noticed a hole about the diameter of a quarter appear at the top. The aperture emitted a beam of vibrant green light into the sky like a searchlight. *Damn,* she thought. *Not what I thought it would do.*

Frustration began to simmer, the need to deactivate the orb overwhelming all else in her mind. She recalled her conversation with Cipher in the chart room on the *Daedalus*, when she'd proposed the invocation theory.

Locating a combination of sigils, Doc pressed her fingertips over all of them simultaneously, the shapes brightly aglow with the same emerald light in the eyes of the *draug*. Then she found what she believed to be the character at the end of this pictorial alphabet.

The Martian *Z*. The extraterrestrial omega.

Her thumb pressed gently over its carved surface. There was an internal *click*, the hole in the top closed, and the two halves of the sphere snapped shut with an abrupt electronic whine. The light ceased to glow and pulse, alien symbols going dark at last.

"I think that's done it," she announced breathlessly. "I think I shut it off."

Amaruq took over holding Deadeye for warmth as Jack stood to take in the approaching Silver Star reinforcements.

"That's good, Doc," he said. "But now we need to deal with them." He could hear the sputter of Model T engines, which meant they'd be in weapon range soon, and that state of affairs would be less than ideal.

"We can't let them have the artifact," Doc insisted, finding no argument among the group.

Jack hugged his arms around his own shoulders for warmth. "We've got a burning ship and frozen sea on one side, endless ice behind us, and the enemy approaching from the front. I'm open to suggestions."

Without thinking, Doc said, "Grenade?" and Jack instantly opened his mouth in protest, but then reconsidered.

"Hang on," he mused. "You might have something." Jack stood and reached to his left hip, where he found the second of the two grenades he'd secured to his belt before they'd arrived at the icebound *Lougen*. Leaving it in place, he turned to Doc, cupping his hands at her chest. "I'm gonna need these," he said, enjoying the brief look of shock and crimson blush to her cheeks as he grabbed the two frag grenades from her harness. "Thanks," he added, winking.

Rushing to the foot of the ice slope at the bow of the ship, Jack located a small crevasse the diameter of a baseball running east-west. *This will do nicely,* he thought. Pulling the first pin, he carefully placed the grenade into the divot and backed away in a hurry. "Fire in the hole!" Then, in quick succession, he pulled the second and third pins and set each grenade in the trough about twenty feet apart.

Everyone ducked into a human pile on top of the shivering Charlie, and the grenade did what it was supposed to do.

The explosion ripped a trough in the ice, prying apart the existing crevasse, creating a deep fissure which ran a good forty yards along the east-west seam.

Within moments, the area surrounding the crew had sheared away from the shoreline, sending them adrift among the other fragmented floes.

Still the Silver Star pushed forward toward the breach, and Jack realized the field radio was still on the back of the Dugdale, on the far side of the *Lougen.* The ship was dancing in flames and billowing dark smoke as it broke completely free of the ice and the main deck washed beneath the water's surface.

A single pale figure stood on the deck, staring out at the stranded crew with piercing green lights for eyes. Amaruq clutched Deadeye as she watched the ship creak and dip slowly beneath the water, taking the reanimated form of Sten with it.

Jack made a quick inventory: three more-or-less able-bodied crew, one suffering acute hypothermia, who needed to get warmed up as soon as possible. One Springfield 1903 rifle, empty. One Winchester 1894 carbine, two shots left. A pair of nickel-plated Colt .45 automatics, each holding one of the last two remaining magazines. Doc's .38 police revolver, four shots left in her spare cylinder.

The Silver Star snow crawlers pulled to a halt just shy of the break in the ice, and soldiers in white parkas began piling out of the vehicles, readying their trench sweepers. The four on the ice floe had achieved some distance, but were still within range of an MP-18, let alone sixteen of them.

"Not to be maudlin," Jack said, hugging the group together around Deadeye's quaking form, "but if we don't get out of this, I've really enjoyed working with you all."

"Oh shut up," Doc admonished, pulling Jack to her and planting a passionate kiss on his wind-chapped lips.

As the *Lougen* finally drifted completely beneath the surface of the Arctic Ocean, each member of the group closed their eyes and braced for the chatter of automatic guns and the impact of bullets. But the sound that met their ears was a much larger staccato.

Jack peered over Deadeye's head and across the water. The *Daedalus* had appeared from the west and opened the forward Lewis guns, strafing down the line of vehicles and men as it raced across overhead.

A succession of explosions amid the snow crawlers on the ground told Jack that whoever wasn't flying the ship had just dropped a box of frag grenades from the gondola door. The assault sent the agents into a blind panic, but any action was ultimately futile. The ice beneath them fragmented in spectacular fashion, sending the four trucks and sixteen enemy soldiers splashing and sputtering to a cold, watery grave.

As the *Daedalus* came around to them, descending over the ice to allow boarding without having to lower the chain ladder, Sparks' smiling face appeared in the gondola door. "Need a ride?" she asked with a colossal grin.

As they hauled Charlie into the main saloon and each followed in turn, Jack was never so happy to have a crew who refused to obey orders.

- CHAPTER 21 -

The hotel accommodations in Nuuk were far from glamorous, but the beds were comfortable, the pub next door was warm and inviting, and they poured an honest drink. They spent the first twenty-four hours after arrival sound asleep in their respective rooms.

The next morning two telegrams arrived. One was to Amaruq from Dr. Eric Bjornson at Copenhagen University. The other was to Jack, from AEGIS command via the London bureau. It was encoded, and referred to an atmospheric disturbance recorded at six degrees south latitude, one hundred forty-three degrees west longitude, which had occurred just prior to 2300 hours two days previous.

Initially confused at why AEGIS would be informing him of a seemingly random atmospheric event halfway around the world, it eventually occurred to him that the coordinates were in the South Pacific, and more specifically, the location of Noble's Isle. The local time corresponded to 6:58 a.m. in Greenland, roughly the moment of Doc's first attempt to shut down the artifact, which sent up a completely different signal instead.

Jack thought it interesting, though there was nothing to be done at the moment.

Doc felt a bit more trepidation about what she might have done, albeit accidentally. She was still relatively new at this closing-interdimensional-portals-and-shutting-down-alien-artifacts work. Ultimately, they didn't know what they didn't know, and until that changed, it was useless to worry.

That didn't stop her from worrying, of course.

As the crew gathered for their final night before departing for Edinburgh, sharing a meal of local reindeer stew and imported Danish beer, they broke off into three small side conversations.

Deadeye regaled Sparks with the tale of the battle against the fearsome polar bears, which had doubled in size in the telling, and possibly had supernatural powers. In return, she spun the exciting yarn about facing down a fighter plane while hanging out the top hatch with only a Tommy gun, which Deadeye had to admit was just about the most exciting tale he'd ever heard.

Cipher extended her condolences to Amaruq for the loss of Sten, and voiced the hope that they might return to *Bålgard,* if their latest contact with the outside world hadn't put them off such interactions for good. Jack and Doc talked shop and plans with Ellen, and traded occasional mushy looks.

Amaruq was the first to address the group. "I'm going back to Copenhagen," she announced.

Doc brightened. "The university?"

"Yes," Amaruq nodded. "Professor Bjornson has been tasked by AEGIS Command to organize their official Occult Studies program. I'm going to help create the syllabus."

"Say, that's just swell," Jack grinned, having returned to his default gosh-and-golly state after the stress of the past week had worn off. "I'm sure we'll be coming to visit, if Doc has her way."

"I dunno," Doc shrugged. "Summer in Denmark could be just the thing."

When the crew was finally full and plenty tipsy, everyone staggered back to their rooms and found their last uninterrupted night of sleep. Jack and Doc fell into their soft but awkwardly-small bed, made love until the small hours of the morning, then napped until

4 a.m. Despite the lack of sound slumber, Jack was energized and ready to go, and Doc reflected that anticipation, excited to get to Scotland and reunite with their daughter.

They assembled at the airfield as a pale sun rose into a stark gray sky. A few locals stood watching. One or two waved as the electric turbofans whirred to speed and the *Daedalus* slipped her mooring cables, rising gracefully into the crisp autumn sky over Greenland.

Cipher was sent to rest in her quarters. Sparks reported all systems were in the green. Deadeye reported from the comms station that the route was clear, no major weather events all the way to Scotland.

Jack glanced over his shoulder from the pilot's chair and shared a knowing look with Doc. These missions were getting more dangerous all the time, and it was harder to leave their little girl, who wouldn't be little much longer. Strangely enough, they agreed that they'd much rather be together as a family, even if it meant facing world-ending peril.

At least they could face it together. And Ellen could see heroism, seat-of-the-pants problem solving, and fearless self-sacrifice modeled by the people she loved most in the world.

They couldn't keep the darkness from her forever. The sooner she learned practical ways to defend herself and others, the better. Because Ellen had to survive, to carry on the fight when her parents and their friends were too old or enfeebled, or dead.

She had to survive, to bear that torch.

She simply *had to*.

༝

The moon hung in an ivory crescent over Paris, the city alive with music and electric light. As the last train pulled into the Gare de Lyon station from La Rochelle, the passengers disembarked like bubbles in a saucer of champagne. It was late, and there were families to greet, parties to attend, lovers to rendezvous with.

As travelers and businessmen pushed through the station, scurrying to and fro, one figure strode slowly and with purpose through the throng of humanity. Endless taxicabs lined the curb outside the station, whisking their fares away to various locales in the City of Lights.

The figure stood at the curb, tall and statuesque, obscured in a long coat and wide-brimmed black hat.

She didn't have to wait long.

Within moments, a shiny new black Rolls Royce Phantom pulled to a stop in front of the station, and a young chauffeur stepped out of the front to open the rear suicide door nearest the curb. The man bowed, offering a hand as the woman approached.

"Master Crowley anticipated your arrival, Madame," he offered in a soft, French-accented tone. "He awaits you at the St. James."

The woman slid into the rear seat, allowing the chauffeur to secure the door.

"Good," said Maria Blutig, lips pursed conspiratorially. "I have much to tell him."

The End

ABOUT THE AUTHOR

Todd Downing's love affair with pulp adventure dates back to his consumption of classic radio dramas and comic books as a child in the 1970s, which broadened into a general appreciation for scifi and fantasy media of all kinds.

He grew up in the greater San Francisco Bay Area, writing and drawing from a young age, his works ever-present in school literary journals and newspapers, and eventually on film. He married his high school sweetheart and moved to Seattle in 1991 where he began to write professionally, and worked as an artist in the videogame industry until his publishing company became a full time operation, while raising two children amid the chaos.

As the co-founder and creative director of Deep7 Press, Downing is the primary author and designer of over fifty roleplaying titles, including *Arrowflight, Grimmworld, Airship Daedalus*, and the official *Red Dwarf* RPG. He continues to write genre fiction for stage, film, comics, audio, and adventure gaming products.

Widowed to cancer in 2005, Downing remarried in 2009 and currently enjoys an empty nest in Port Orchard, Washington, with his wife, the neighbors' visiting cat, and a flock of unruly chickens.

Join the author's mailing list at:
www.todddowning.com

More *Airship Daedalus* & *AEGIS Tales* content:
www.airshipdaedalus.com

Read the previous adventures of the
Airship *Daedalus:*
A Shield Against the Darkness
(Book #1)
Assassins of the Lost Kingdom
(Book #2, by E.J. Blaine)
The Golden City
(Book #3)
Legend of the Savage Isle
(Book #4)

Plus:
AEGIS Tales
A retro-pulp anthology, volume 1

Primordial Soup Kitchen
A Collection of Short Strangeness

AVAILABLE NOW!

Made in the USA
Monee, IL
03 February 2025

11461194R00156